MW00744327

Inheritance

Inheritance

Kirsten Gundlack

QUATTRO BOOKS

The publication of *Inheritance* has been generously supported by the Canada Council for the Arts and the Ontario Arts Council.

 Canada Council **Conseil des Arts**
for the Arts du Canada

 ONTARIO ARTS COUNCIL
CONSEIL DES ARTS DE L'ONTARIO
50 YEARS OF ONTARIO GOVERNMENT SUPPORT OF THE ARTS
50 ANS DE SOUTIEN DU GOUVERNEMENT DE L'ONTARIO AUX ARTS

Author's photograph: Dahlia Katz
Cover painting: Leah Murray
Cover design: Sarah Beaudin
Editor: John Calabro
Typography: Grey Wolf Typography

Library and Archives Canada Cataloguing in Publication

Gundlack, Kirsten
     Inheritance / Kirsten Gundlack.

Also issued in electronic format.
ISBN 978-1-927443-35-4

     I. Title.

PS8613.U567I54 2013   C813'.6   C2013-900396-7

Published by Quattro Books Inc.
382 College Street
Toronto, Ontario, M5T 1S8
www.quattrobooks.ca

Printed in Canada

JASON CALLS. IT'S EARLY, and hot. At this hour Grace will be cleaving the water of their pool, blading through her morning lengths. Usually he holds out the receiver so that I can hear the splashing. If the girls are up they will yell COME SWIM! into the phone.

But Jason sounds vacant, his voice strangely airless. He tells me an impossible thing about Grace: that she died this morning. Collapsed on the deck.

No, I tell him, because I spoke to my sister yesterday and yesterday still counts. I want him to start the call again. Instead he tells me about an image they showed him a little while ago at the hospital: Grace's brain with too much white. He didn't understand the image, but the faces of the doctors showing it to him told him what it meant.

Jason, I say. He needs to start over. He sounds like something in him has detached and fallen away. I am talking to a man cut in half, looking down in wonder at the place where his torso ends. How is any of this possible? How is he still alive?

He asks me how in God's name he'll tell the girls.

Something in me detaches, and falls away.

Aneurysm.

Aneurysm.

Aneurysm.

Even before Grace died I didn't like the word. Etymology aside, I don't think the shape of it is properly suited to the meaning. I keep repeating it but the sound continues to suggest other definitions.

Aneurysm: a narrow fissure in rock.

Aneurysm: a meandering waterway.

Aneurysm: an ideological conundrum.

It could mean any of these things, but it doesn't. An aneurysm is a vascular puzzle. It is the name of the hidden Gordian knot in Grace's brain that solved the problem of itself yesterday morning with a single cataclysmic burst. She was thirty-five. I am twenty-nine. Not one thing about this is right. I have been waiting since yesterday for events to slip back onto the proper track, to return us to the present we are supposed to be in. The longer we continue to move in this direction the more likely it seems that we're stuck this way, going forward without Grace, and I have no idea how to do that.

Jump cut: I am in Jon's car. Since Jason's call I have been choked and helpless, relying on others to hand me around like so much cargo. My roommate Fumie took me to the train in Kingston and my sister Bianca got me from the station to the Holiday Inn here in town. Now Jon, a close friend since vet college, is driving me over to Grace and Jason's house. Their lawyer needs to talk to me. He says it's urgent, but nothing is urgent now as far as I'm concerned. The emergency is over and it ended badly.

Still the lawyer insisted we meet as soon as possible. *The clock is ticking on this,* he told me over the phone, but he wouldn't say what *this* was.

For a long time my calming mantra has been the Latin of the body. *Epicranius frontalis, occipitus.* Connected by the *epicranial aponeurosis. Temporalis,* above the ear. *Orbicularis oculi,* helps you blink. *Buccinator. Zygomaticus. Orbicularis oris,* the pucker muscle. *Platysma. Masseter.* Good words, smooth as old wood.

"Libera me Domine de morte aeterna in die illa tremenda," Jon says. "Quando coeli movendi sunt et terra."

Jon likes his altar-boy Latin. We used to do this together at school to steady ourselves before exams: body parts for me and Requiem mass for him, back and forth. At first he called it my pretentious Latin tic but eventually it became our mutual habit. We both like this exchange of living systems and verses for the dead, the way the words entwine.

Jon wants to keep reminding me that he's here. After Fumie called him about Grace he came without being asked, drove all the way down from Sudbury after working a night shift. He arrived expecting to find me screaming or catatonic, not in this worrying Purgatorial midway state. I am listening and speaking to him as if from a long, long way off. I cannot yet understand that Grace is gone. Worse than the shock I'm feeling now is the dread of a bigger reckoning just over the hill, the moment when it finally sinks in that she really is dead. It's like knowing in only the most abstract way how much my torn-up limb will hurt when the freezing wears off. I might go crazy with pain; I might die of shock. I might, I might.

The car smells are male human, wet dog, old fry grease, heated vinyl. At stoplights Jon bangs on the dash, trying to Fonzie the AC back to life. He says that even dawn in Sudbury was warm. He came in with what he was wearing when he left the clinic – t-shirt from a bungee-jumping outfit in Wakefield, cargo shorts, Crocs – and now he's looking down and frowning at himself.

"Shit, Hellie, I'm sorry. This isn't appropriate. I don't even have pants on, for Christ's sake."

Some part of me registers this as funny, because the Jon I first met thought appropriate was everyone else's problem. If I wasn't so far away I'd remind him of this. He has also apologized for not showering yet. Animal me is breathing him in, stupidly happy to have him so close. She wants to climb onto his lap and bury her face in his armpit. *Bring on the eccrine stink*, she declares. *If it's his it's good.*

Animal me is the one being inappropriate. I want to kill all my responses, conscious and not, but animal me seems unkillable. Maybe I should be glad of that.

Jon brakes and a pile of junk slides forward from underneath my seat. I reach down to push it back and my fingers encounter the handled case of a dog lead. I pick it up and balance it on my palm. Jon glances over, sees what I'm holding and groans.

"Goddammit. I told Leanne that was at the house."

"Schuster's with Leanne?"

"Sort of. She wouldn't take him at her place because he's such a stinky bastard, but she said she'd go over and let him out."

Schuster is Jon's yellow Labrador. In the summer months he makes the car smell like a stagnant pond and refuses to ride anywhere but shotgun. According to Jon I am the only passenger who has ever welcomed Schuster's hundred pounds of wiggly dank dogflesh on my lap. We adore each other, Schuster and I, and right now it would feel so good to wrap my arms around his reassuringly solid bulk and rest my cheek against his smelly back. Austin, my border collie, is at home with Fumie and I hate having to go dogless for any length of time.

"You could have brought him," I say, but Jon shakes his head.

"Nah. He's too hyper and the car's too hot. Leanne'll take care of him."

He sounds doubtful. Leanne, the latest in Jon's long series of high maintenance girlfriends, has a marked dislike of all dogs bigger than handbag size. She can't fathom Jon's affection for sloppy, klutzy Schuster any more than she can understand his friendship with me. In Leanne's world pets and companions are nothing if not good accessories, and Jon's dog and I are not exactly image-builders. Schuster is an expression of Jon's weakness for animals, and I, the mangled little friend – well, now, what am I? Jon's pity project? The object of a hidden fetish? Leanne can't figure it out. She won't look at me if she can possibly help it, but when Jon talks to me on Skype she makes a point of floating around the living room behind him wearing one of his shirts and nothing else. From my end it looks like he's being haunted by the ghost of a dead sorority president.

I get it, I always want to tell her: she owns his ass. Well, I hauled that slightly dyslexic ass along from the first day of undergrad at Guelph to the last day of veterinary college and saw to it that we both got our Doctor of Veterinary Medicine. If Leanne owns Jon's ass then I own his brain. His heart is anybody's guess.

Jon's left hand is resting on his knee, right hand at four o'clock on the steering wheel. As a courtesy he asked me if I wanted to drive even though it's obvious that I'm too messed up. He knows I prefer to have him sitting to my right, to spare him what he affectionately calls the Dora Maar side of my face. Only Jon would come up with a nickname like that and use it in public. When he started with it he wasn't trying to be kind or derogatory or clever, he was simply remarking upon what he saw as my striking similarity to the fragmented face paintings of Picasso's mistress. It explained his calm in the face of my face; if my Dora struck him as ugly it was a familiar ugly. Artistic, in its own way.

I don't especially care for most of the Dora pieces, but I can't deny the resemblance. From the right I look almost normal, if you squint, but the Dora-view from the left is decidedly unlovely and my stupid vanity wants lovely for Jon. Apparently my vanity is unkillable, too. I wonder if I've kept anything useful.

"Besides," Jon says, almost to himself, "I don't think your folks would enjoy seeing us pull up with you and my big ol' dog in the car together. Not what they need right now."

He tilts the wheel, steering with his thumb and forefinger. I mouth the names of the forearm muscles: *extensor carpi ulnaris, flexor carpi ulnaris, extensor digitorum.*

"Requiem æternam dona eis, Domine," Jon says. "Amen."

At the stoplight he looks me over carefully, checking for fresh cracks.

"It's okay to pray, Hellie," he says. "I did."

People are assembling at the house that is now just Jason's and the girls'. Where does that impulse come from? No number of guests will fill the sudden Grace-shaped void, but it seems to be pulling them in towards itself like the vortex of a drowned ship.

In the kitchen we find Milton, Grace's Sheltie, raiding the garbage. Food has been put out along the counter, mostly pasta in oblong pans. People ask us, apologizing, if we know where they can find a serving spoon for their casserole because they forgot to bring theirs. News of Grace's death has triggered a neighbourhood-wide casserole-making reflex but no one has thought to bring disposable plates or cutlery. Jon says the same thing happened at his mother's house after his dad died. "I'll go," he says, and whistles for Milton. "Who wants a car ride?"

After they leave I wander, avoiding people. I don't want to join any of the groups that have formed around the first floor and patio, and I don't see the lawyer. Jason is circulating wearily through the house, carrying Georgia and leading Millie. He has not slept. Visitors tell him how sorry they are for his loss and he says the same thing back. Millie and Georgia cannot be cajoled into speaking. They stay big-eyed and silent, keeping white-tight grips on their daddy. When people aren't talking with Grace's family they give them a wide berth, exchanging looks with each other as Jason and the girls pass.

Somewhere in the house my father is standing in a corner watching my mother hold court, and if I wasn't so selfish I'd go find them. At this moment a proper daughter would be with my sisters Diana and Bianca playing footman to Mother's grief, but I don't have the stomach for it. My mother doesn't need a reason to be pitied; as far as I know she has yet to meet anyone more deserving of sympathy than herself. Out of all of us I was by far the closest to Grace, but she will insist that her mother's pain is infinitely greater and more important than anyone else's. In the background my neglected father will allow himself to be forgotten, thinking up reasons why he is to blame for all of this. I don't have the stomach for that, either.

On the dining room table someone has piled the wrapped bodies of bouquets, dozens of them. Some have been hastily dumped into vases of water. The heads on a large bunch of peonies are nodding, blown wide open by the heat.

I can't stand, I can't sit. I feel as if I've been flayed: everything hurts. I don't know where to direct my eyes. Wherever I look, the ordinary things of Grace and Jason's family life strike me as frivolous and useless. What does this fucking lawyer want? If it's about money, if it's not truly urgent, I will bash in his head with one of these vases.

Oh, anger. That's what's next. I am crushing the head of a peony in my hand as I construct the sound of lead crystal against a lawyer's skull. Not too wooden, not too crisp, but there must be a distinct *kunk* as the bone divides. I felt and heard the bones of my face crack like that once. I've never wondered before what it would feel like to do it to someone else.

"Helena?"

I look up. An enormous man is standing over me, and he is not prepared for the Dora Maar view. His face suffers an involuntary spasm of expression that he kills immediately. I suppose lawyers have to be good at that.

Arthur-the-lawyer has found me, and he is immense. His skull is much too far away. The peony is a dead wet bundle in the centre of my palm.

We climb the stairs to the third-floor office, Grace's tree fort. A view of the pool, blue-sky wallpaper, preschooler art and shelves of poetry. Grace was an amateur Walt Whitman scholar. From the window I can see tent caterpillars in the apple tree.

Arthur fills the room, making everything in it feel closer and darker. He is too tall to stand anywhere but in the centre where the sloped ceiling is highest. He refuses the rocker, saying he'll break it, and takes the ottoman instead. Even sitting he's two heads taller than me.

He can't express how sorry he is for my loss. Sorry too for having to draw my attention to this urgent matter, but my final decision will be needed within twenty-four hours. He hopes I'll understand. Still sweating from the climb, he looms over me while I sign a document saying I won't disclose to anyone what I'm about to read. He takes it back, puts an envelope into my hands and gets up. "I'll be downstairs if you have questions. Take your time."

The envelope I am left alone to open is legal-length, recycled grey, CONFIDENTIAL and URGENT stamped on its face in red. *Helena Hallett* is written in Grace's loopy script across the front and the seal on the back is signed *F. Grace Hallett-Fraser*. Loath to disturb Grace's signature, I slit the top with scissors and pull out a thin clutch of documents.

DIRECTED ORGAN DONATION for F. GRACE HALLETT-FRASER

It is my wish that, upon my death, my organs be donated for medical use. I hereby direct my attorneys to make known to the appropriate medical professionals the following directed donations:

a) WITH THE EXCEPTION OF MY FACE
(see designation below) my organs and tissues are to be offered on the basis of most appropriate recipient/most immediate need at the time of my death...

I put the paper down, run my wrist across my eyes and pick it up again.

Highlighted:

b) WITH REGARD TO THE TISSUES OF MY FACE
(designated for these purposes as all necessary bone, cartilage, superficial and deep tissues covering the area of my skull superior to both clavicles and anterior to the coronal plane, including the scalp), my sister HELENA HALLETT is hereby granted sole right of refusal to any or all of said tissues.

Back from the supermarket, Jon comes upstairs with his shopping and finds me sitting on the floor of Grace's study with a sheaf of creased and damp papers in my hand. He takes them from me and feels my forehead. He produces a bottle of Gatorade from his bag and wraps my fingers around it. In times of emotional crisis, Jon's first instinct is to balance electrolytes.

"Hydrate. Then we'll talk." He frowns at the papers. "Is this a will?"

I shake my head.

"Can I look?" He starts flipping through the pages without waiting for a response, and I decide that this doesn't count as me disclosing anything. I hold the bottle of glowworm-green fluid to my neck and watch his lips move as he reads. He goes down to the bottom of the directed donation form and stops. Goes back. Reads it again and looks up at me.

Jon prides himself on being difficult to surprise. I think it's a dumb thing to be proud of, so it's always a little gratifying to see him caught off-guard. Now he is in open-mouthed shock.

"Hellie, do you see what this says? Do you *get* this?"

"Yes."

"Your sister left you her face."

"Yes." I am nauseated. I think it's an assimilation problem. "But why?"

"Why what?"

"Why did she do that?"

Jon stares at me, at the exposed ruin of eye and nose and lip that my hair has fallen away from. That is his wordless reply. How can I not know why?

*/ */ */

"If you could have anyone's face, whose would you choose?"

It was either a teenaged Diana or Bianca who brought it up first, I forget which. When we were children both twin sisters liked to start rounds of what-if games at dinner, but their questions were opposite in character. Bianca favoured expansive best-case scenarios in which we dreamed up uses for our limitless wealth and freedom: diseases we would wipe out, stars for our blockbuster films, all the countries in which we would have houses. Diana, on the other hand, liked situations where we had to make tough choices. She was stricter about her parameters than Bianca, and her questions were a good deal more grim. What if we could only keep one limb? Would we rather be trapped underwater, underground, or in space? Which sense could we stand to lose?

To Bianca it was all lighthearted fun, but to Diana it was deathly serious. One night I angered her by refusing to answer when she demanded to know which pet we would save from a house fire. She wanted me to choose only one, but I wouldn't. I was a child at the time, and the question distressed me so much that when she pressed me further I left the table in tears.

"Oh, for Heaven's *sake*, Hellie," she said in disgust as I got up. "It's only a *question*."

"A question about letting animals die, Diana," I heard Daddy say. "Must you always provoke?"

In the twins' what-if questions lay the essential difference in their perspectives: possibilities versus constraints. The face question was interesting because it might have come from either of them, looks-obsessed creatures that they were then.

But it was Grace who had actually gotten the ball rolling by bringing up the new directed donation legislation while we were getting dinner on the table. She was writing a paper on it for her second-year bioethics course and wanted opinions for and against.

"Against," Mother said. "Selfish, selfish, being allowed to give to your family first. How did such a thing ever get legalized?"

"Precedent," Grace said. "Gaetan vs. the Province of Ontario. It's been legal in the States for years."

"Not all states," Daddy said. "And the ruling could be overturned. It might not last here."

"Maybe, but you should all be extra nice to me just in case," Grace said. "I have very high-quality lungs."

"Yeah, I think I read that on a bathroom wall somewhere," Diana said, and Bianca snickered. I didn't laugh. I wasn't quite a teenager yet and didn't really get it. Besides, I refused to make fun of Grace.

"What about heart?" Daddy said. "You've probably got the strongest heart in the family, what with all the swimming. That's what I'd want."

"Eugene," Mother said, but we girls laughed and shivered. Delicious, these gory topics. A little game ensued: whose organs were the best? In addition to Grace's lungs and heart we awarded First Place to Bianca's kidneys, Diana's corneas, my liver, Mother's powerful larynx. Daddy reckoned that he wasn't good for spare parts anymore. Then Mother said it was time to say grace and would we please leave off our discussion while people had food in their mouths.

On to the question, which I now recall was Diana's. Dinner had been served and the six of us were relatively quiet for the moment, concentrating on our first forkfuls. Diana surveyed the table and announced that she had tonight's question, "which taps into the *zeitgeist.*"

At sixteen Diana was very, very full of herself. Grace, who had taught her the word *zeitgeist*, rolled her eyes. But Daddy, cheeks bulging, shrugged and gestured with his fork: go ahead.

"Further to the topic of family organ donations," Diana said, "you will recall that skin is the body's largest organ. Theoretically it is possible, under the new legislation, for an individual to donate his or her face to a relative. So if you could ask any family member to leave you his or her face, whose would you want?"

"That's enough," Mother snapped. She said she thought she had made it clear that this was not suitable dinnertime conversation. Plus it was Personally Sensitive to Certain Family Members, thus unacceptable in any context. This last said with the barest glance at me.

"Sensitive?" Grace said. She was staring at Diana, wide-eyed with outrage on my behalf. "Fucking *in*sensitive, more like. What is *wrong* with you?"

"And for that you may leave the table, Grace," Mother said. But Grace was already out of her seat. As she picked up her plate she bumped Diana's glass with her elbow, sloshing water over Diana's dinner roll.

"That's all right," Diana said. She picked up her bread plate and took it to the sink. When she returned to the table she was smiling. "Sorry, Mother, Daddy. I didn't mean to cause a fuss."

"The hell you didn't," Daddy said. "The subject is closed, ladies. Are we all clear on that?"

But the seed had been planted. The unsettling notion of such a thing actually being within one's grasp was too intriguing not to think about. Yet at the time we were much too young and the idea was far too big to feel like it might ever matter to us. I knew that doctors had floated the idea of a total facial allograft for me after I stopped growing, "if all else failed" – but I also knew that my parents would never consider such a thing under any circumstances. So even to me, everything around the face-choice question had possibility but none of it seemed real. Human face transplants sounded like futurist fiction, legalities were dull abstractions, and death was the biggest fable of all.

I still wonder what Diana's motive was for that question. The twins and I knew without asking one another that three of us would have the same answer. The only mystery was what Grace's choice would be.

If it hadn't been for me, we Halletts would have been thought of as a family of great beauties. The three older ones were sometimes talked about that way, although honesty compels me to point out that the twins were merely pretty and it was Grace's halo effect which made them all shine. But the twins saw us in every famous family of girls: the Little Women, Austen's Bennett sisters, the Virgin Suicides, the dancing princesses. They grew into adulthood believing the Hallett sisters were possessed of a special beauty that really only belonged to Grace.

In this context "the Hallett sisters" didn't really mean me, of course. As a Hallett girl I got to ride along with the others, but my appearance set me apart early on. Luckily for others, I was one of four daughters and could easily be included in group flattery: *look at these lovely young ladies*. There weren't many occasions in my youth where someone had to summon a compliment just for me. If I had been in the position of advising them I would have suggested that they stick to hair – I had glorious hair – or clothes. *What a pretty dress* brought smiles to all present; false-hearty exclamations of *don't you look beautiful, Helena!* made everyone flinch. When people did this it felt to me like we were all attempting a group act of imagination, trying for my sake to superimpose what might have been over what was. I played along, but we all looked foolish. Ignoring the fact of Dora never worked.

It's all right, I always wanted to say. I know what I look like.

When I was two and a half I was attacked by a dog at a park and suffered extensive damage to about seventy percent of my face, including the entire left side. My mother always told the story as an if-only lament: if only she hadn't left me in my father's care that morning.

If only he hadn't taken me to the park.

If only he had taken me in his arms, instead of leaving me in the stroller.

If only I had been sitting still instead of waving, laughing, grasping at things, drawing the dog's attention.

If only the dog had been stopped before he got to my stroller.

If only he had taken me by the arm instead.

If only he had been subdued before he could sink his teeth into my face, pull me from the stroller, shake me, drop me, pick me up, renew his grip on me half a dozen times. If only he hadn't been so crazed, so big, so impossible to constrain. If only my father and the dog's owner had not been so frightened. If only the man with the baseball bat had come over sooner.

But one could go on and on like this almost indefinitely, picking apart the strands of Fate's web. Where should it stop? My mother decided, ultimately, that it might as well stop with me. If only, if only, if *only* Helena hadn't unwittingly done whatever it was that so enraged the dog that day. For surely, my mother said, I must have done something.

For all these years I have retained one memory from the attack. I have never told either of my parents about it, because my father still worries (and my mother assumes) that I have some fragmented impression of Daddy helplessly wringing his hands as I am mauled. But I don't. I don't remember my father there, or anyone else. I remember nothing of being pulled from the stroller and shaken, nothing of onlookers screaming or my blood spattering the ground. I have no recollection of pain, or terror; I have no sense of self in my memory at all.

What I have is the extraordinary heat of the dog's mouth, and its fear: a blazing, blinding, end-of-world fear that leapt like flame in the eye inches from my own. I have one flash of that terrified eye, of knotty pink veins on white sclera exposed as the eyeball rolled in its socket, and an overwhelming sense that the dog was in pain. At that moment that dog's psychic agony seemed to me to be infinitely greater than any earthly pain its bite could inflict. It still haunts me. Throughout my life, whenever anyone has shown the least amount of pity for what I went through, I have always thought of that terrible fear and how very much I wanted to help that dog.

The only funny story associated with the attack concerns Grace, who was nearly nine at the time. When my parents brought her and the six-year-old twins to see me at the hospital three days after my admission, Diana and Bianca shrieked at the sight of my swollen purple patchwork face and hid behind my mother. While they were being consoled Grace stepped up to the edge of the bed and conducted an unflinching appraisal of my injuries. "Whoo, Daddy," she said, and sighed. "That is gonna be one pain in the ass to fix."

Out of the mouths of babes. From that point on my childhood – and my parents' lives – revolved around trips to various children's hospitals and pediatric specialists and offices of maxillofacial surgeons, intersections through which children like me travelled with two-inch-thick medical files. We all bore the obvious effects of something: a single injury (BB gun pellet to the eye, smashed mandible from a jungle-gym fall) or larger-scale damage (garage fire, toboggan vs. tree), and we all had a story. I learned to recognize the more commonplace injuries and piece together the events behind them, but occasionally in a hospital corridor we would pass a child whose story could not even be guessed at.

"Lord," my mother would gasp when we weren't even out of earshot, making me cringe. "What on Earth could have done *that*?"

It didn't occur to her to speculate on what the other kid's parents thought about the child *they* had just passed in the hall. She never seemed to hear them saying exactly the same things about me.

My own story seemed pretty simple: dog attack with post-op complications – lots of complications. By second grade I could describe them knowledgeably enough, having heard my parents explain to each new surgeon all that had gone wrong in the ER and the weeks following my admission to hospital: this doctor's lack of experience, that one's poor choice of technique, the repeated tissue infections, the osteomyelitis in my jaw, the grafts that would not take. The result was a kid collage made with runny glue, a Raggedy Helena with half a smile.

Additional surgeries in my teens and early twenties brought slight improvements, but in my public-school years my appearance was downright unsettling. I'm not complaining about everything; a few of the early grafts took well and the prosthetic part of my jaw has held up brilliantly. Generally, though, I was decidedly unlucky with those early rounds of reconstruction. By my tenth birthday the borrowed cartilage of my nose was caving in. My brow had begun to slip, the connective tissue underneath slowly relinquishing its hold on damaged muscle. The makeshift left eyelid that had replaced the original was badly constructed and I didn't yet have a scleral shell to hide the strange scarring across my eyeball. That damned eyelid wouldn't close properly, either, and scar tissue around the eye had contracted to give it a peculiar dragged-down appearance. There were ongoing sinus issues, problems with my nose-breathing and the punctured part of my hard palate. Grafted facial skin had thinned to the point where it was clinging tissue-like to my teeth, my molars visible in high relief through my cheek. Diana and Bianca complained to my parents that they couldn't stand watching me eat.

But not Grace; Grace never minded. In fact, it was Grace who came up with our little lunch game, one we played only when it was just the two of us: I would take a mouthful of something and she had to guess what it was from the shape that she saw through the skin of my cheek. Following later surgeries I was finally able to relish the crunch of celery between my teeth without worrying that it might poke right through my face, but I'll never again taste that watery green without a thrill of memory-pain. For a moment Grace is resurrected, rolling with laughter in her seat.

"Celery?" she shrieked. Grace was a shrieker. "That's your big mystery item, *celery*? Hellie, it's *ribbed*!"

Grace said that if I was going to be any good at this kind of subterfuge I would have to practice religiously in front of a mirror. I don't like mirrors, but for Grace I practiced. Never fooled her on celery but I did fine-tune a technique for camouflaging whole macaroni. When Daddy caught us playing and asked us what the point of our little game was, Grace told him that she was training me up to be a drug mule.

Well, Daddy got mad. He said that it wasn't even remotely funny. Our game was macabre and disgusting and it made light of my injuries. Clearly Grace had no respect for her sister's suffering, which disappointed him. He expected her to apologize to me and didn't want to see us engaged in this kind of activity again.

After he left the room Grace said, "Hellie, I respect your suffering." She was trying on a fake-serious baritone that cracked.

I giggled. "Then I respect your respect."

"And *I* respect *your* respect of my respect, Hellie."

"And *I* respect *your* respect of *my* respect of *your* respect, Grace."

"Enough!" She held out a can of mixed nuts. "Take three. I'll bet you a buck I can guess which kinds they are. And no hiding the edges under your tongue."

◊ ◊ ◊

At the hotel Jon opens my door for me, sits me down on the bed and puts a glass of water in my hand. "Drink," he says. "Don't just hold."

"You always pour water down my throat."

"You always need it."

I drink and watch him poke around the room for a bit, opening and shutting drawers. The hotel has seen less than six months of use and still holds a flat odour of adhesive and paint. The room is done in assembly-line friendly – neutrals, Home Depot prints, featureless dark wood. Comfortable but forgettable, it imposes nothing on me. Staying with family was not an option, psychologically; the clutter and old arguments would have put me over the edge. This is exactly what I need right now: an Everyroom, functional but history-free.

Jon opens the curtains and turns on the air. He lifts my suitcase onto the luggage stand, gets me an extra pillow from the closet and shuffles through the coffee supplies on the bathroom counter. "Tea," he says speculatively, but I shake my head. He gets himself a Coke from the fridge and sits down on the other bed.

"That's a six-dollar Coke, Jon."

He pulls the tab, grimacing. "Then I expect great things from it."

He sits cross-legged on the bed balancing the Coke between his fingertips, looking at me intently. He wants to talk about Grace's bequest but doesn't want to push me.

We left the house in a hurry and didn't speak in the car because I was sure I was about to be violently, spectacularly sick. Now I'm lying back on the bed feeling less inclined to vomit, but still fighting a nasty tilting sensation.

Jon yawns and rubs his cheek. He left Sudbury straight off an ER clinic night shift and he's looking bleary-eyed. "How you doin', Dora?"

"Lie down, Faulkner."

He looks down at the bed. "Here?"

"There."

"Awfully forward of you, but I won't say no." He stretches out, spreading his arms wide. "This why you got two doubles? Making room for me?"

"Two doubles is cheaper."

"You don't say." He yawns again. "You didn't answer me, Hellie. You feeling any better?"

"Better than what?"

"Better than before, when you were standing on puke's precipice."

"I don't know."

"Was that a function of not eating, or an emotional thing?"

"I don't know."

"Both, maybe?"

He's fixing on me. This is the look he uses to get me to deal plainly with him: sympathetic, affectionate, but intense. I think he thinks he's channelling the Force.

"It's a hell of a thing, Helena."

"Mm-hm."

"Did you know she was going to do that?"

I might still throw up. "Mm. No."

"She never talked to you about it?"

"Never."

"So this is totally left field."

"Yes and no."

He waits while I sit up and drink more water. I'm considering whether or not I want to go further into this with him, or anyone. I need a way through this shifting maze of feeling but I don't think it's something anyone else can find for me.

"You don't want to talk about it," he says.

I fix him with my own plain dealer, which on Dora looks as serious as cancer. "What I don't want is to be talked into or out of anything. If you want to go through this with me that's fine, but I don't want to be pushed in a direction. I don't want advice, period. Can you do that?"

"Of course."

"Because you tend to be prescriptive."

"Not this time," he says, sounding wounded.

I am so glad he's here, and so grateful not to be alone. But for once something is taking up more of my bandwidth than he is.

"We did talk about transplants," I say, "but only hypothetically. She had nothing against the idea in general but she didn't think I needed one."

"Is this even doable on short notice? Don't you have to be on a list, or something?"

"I was. Almost."

"Huh?"

"I applied to be on a list. At Sunnybrook."

He's well and truly shocked. "When?"

"Four or five years ago. I got through the first stage of screening and then they told me I might as well forget it."

"Why?"

"Function, mostly. My nose sort of works, my jaw works okay, nothing's open that shouldn't be. My movement and eyesight are manageable. I can chew, my palate's intact and I can speak clearly enough to be understood. Aesthetically my face is considered to be in the low-acceptable range, if you can believe that. Meanwhile, they've got a few dozen catastrophic cases with no matches in sight. So they said I should forget it. I'm never going to be eligible, because there'll always be someone more fucked up than me."

"Sorry," Jon says. "I meant why did you apply for the list?"

I look at him carefully. He appears to be serious. My hair has fallen back, so he's even getting the full Dora right now. Still he waits for an answer.

"Jon, when I said I didn't know why Grace was giving me her face, you gave me that look like the answer was obvious."

"The answer *is* obvious: why wouldn't she? If she thought you wanted it and it might make your life better, why not? I'm guessing she knew about this list."

"She and Jason knew. Nobody else."

"And she knew it wasn't going to happen that way. Because it wouldn't, right?"

No, it would not. Even if I had priority status the odds wouldn't be in my favour. Faces aren't donated as often as other tissues, and there are a lot of variables involved in getting a match. I need a brain-dead female with similar skin tone and a face of roughly the same size, preferably within a couple of decades of my age. Finding a donor with those traits who's also histocompatible with me would be like winning the transplant lottery. Otherwise I'd be looking at a potentially life-shortening regimen of immunosuppressive drugs to minimize the odds of tissue rejection. Grace's directed donation is effectively an end run around every major obstacle standing between me and a new face.

"So did Grace understand the situation, Hellie?"

"Yes."

"And did she have any idea of whether or not she might be a good match?"

"She knew she was. I had a lot of trouble with grafts in the first couple of years after the attack so she offered to donate skin. She got as far as getting typed and then I ended up not needing it."

"Lucky for her. So the typing is close?"

"We're HLA-identical."

"Wow."

"It's not that unusual. One in four odds for siblings, so chances were that one of my sisters would be a match."

"But of course it was Grace," Jon says. "That is poetry, Hellie."

"What is?"

"Even your antigens got along."

I start to laugh. I don't mean to. Jon is completely sincere, and he's right: the symmetry is lovely. I just can't acknowledge how lovely it is without acknowledging that it's gone, so instead I laugh. Jon looks injured.

"You know what I mean," he says, and I cough and sober up and nod.

"So it's doable. She's a good match, she knew that." He's ticking things off on his fingers. "She knew how badly you wanted it, and she knew it wouldn't happen any other way. So where's the uncertainty?"

"It doesn't seem like something she would do."

"Why not?"

"Because she wanted me to be okay with the way I look. That was important to her. She didn't really understand why I wanted to get on the list."

"I don't either," Jon says, "but it's not my life. Maybe she concluded the same thing, that it was your decision and if you wanted it that was good enough for her."

He's so tired. He's locked on to the discussion, focused on me and the problem that I have not really articulated, but his blinks keep getting longer. "So maybe that's why, Hellie. She realized she could give you the chance, so she did."

"Maybe."

"Is it a problem for you, not knowing the exact reason? Because odds are you'll never know."

"Yeah."

"You'd do it for her, wouldn't you?"

"I would."

"There you go," he says. Long blink.

I reach over and touch his outstretched fingers. "Go to sleep, Faulkner. We'll talk later."

"I'm fine." He closes his eyes, his face still turned towards me. "I just need a minute."

After Jon's breathing becomes deep and regular I get up and go into the bathroom, a bright-white subway-tiled cube. It's fearsomely clean and almost pointedly featureless except for two enormous mirrors, one across the wall above the sink and the other on the back of the door. No getting away from my reflection here.

Every once in a while there's a moment when I catch a glimpse of myself from a certain angle and I think that maybe it's not so bad. If I turn the right way and squint, the person I see looks…okay. Not perfect, but okay. Right now, in this bathroom, I am not having one of those moments. These huge, clear-eyed mirrors are excruciatingly honest and the acid wash of the fluorescents doesn't do Dora any favours. In this light even the palest pink looks an unhealthy keloid purple, and the complete absence of shadows makes it appear as though I am missing my left cheekbone and most of my nose. How cheering.

Resigned to seeing my face anyway, I check for rough-day residue: tears, travelling makeup, snot. To be fair to Dora, it's not a great package. Even the normal parts clearly belong to someone who hasn't been sleeping or eating. No wonder poor Arthur shuddered; this hollow-eyed creature must have trumped every dreaded expectation he had about Grace's disfigured sister. I look ancient, battle-scarred and unreachably sad.

Fumie told me recently that she thinks thirty is the first major reckoning point for most people. Thirty, she said, is when you look in the mirror and realize that what you've got is what you've got. There's nothing left to grow out of and not much left to grow into, no superpowers or latent magical abilities have manifested themselves, your extraordinary insight/genius/talent is turning out to be rather ordinary, and it's too late to be a prodigy at anything – if ever you were. You are unequivocally a standard human adult, supposedly at your peak, and life is still hard. Physically and mentally the best you can do is maintain whatever you've got.

When she shared this revelation, Fumie's ulterior motive was to frighten me into joining the gym with her. But I already knew the disappointment she was describing, more intimately than she could have imagined; I had been through it at twenty-four. My surgeon, Dr. Choudry, had worked for nearly a decade to restore as much mobility, shape and symmetry to my face as possible, but inevitably we reached a point beyond which he said I would begin to experience "a sharply diminishing rate of return" on further procedures. I remember him touching Dora lightly with his fingertips as he told me this, trying to soften the message of the words. He had made all the major improvements that were possible at the time; further aesthetic tweaks would be considered elective, unfortunately. But my function was much improved, wasn't it? And the balance of the features – much better, wouldn't I agree?

No, I would not. It was better, yes, but not much. Not enough. I sat there staring straight ahead, glassy-eyed and silent. Dr. Choudry sighed.

"Because you're not a sculpture, Helena. You're not made of rock. Living tissue has limits, it reacts to the trauma of surgery – you know this. Reconstructive medicine has limits. We must have the humility to see this, both of us. Perhaps in the future there will be more options, but for now –" those cool fingertips resting on my cheek, clinical and soothing. "How about a rest? Because you need it, Helena. Your face needs it. Let it be for now."

I didn't doubt that Dr. Choudry was acting in my best interests; he always had. There was also the fact that I was a university student by then, with no money for elective procedures. Outraged by my decision to enter veterinary college, Mother and Daddy were barely speaking to me, so parental help was not an option. Even if the money hadn't been an issue I couldn't have possibly taken any more recovery time from school, especially for surgeries that were unlikely to make much of a difference anyway. I was being forced to accept that what I had at that moment, functionally and aesthetically, was probably the best I could hope for. Barring, of course, the remote possibility of a sudden, radical advancement in reconstructive medicine. Or, remoter still, a transplant.

Up to that point I'd been able to comfort myself with the idea that my face was a work in progress. Waiting for your body to get sorted out is something most teenagers go through regardless of looks, so from that standpoint I wasn't unusual. Other kids had braces and acne to wish away; I had scar tissue and misshapen bone. Like all construction sites it was messy, but I had kept telling myself that once the scaffolding finally came down it would look like a whole new place. Then Dr. Choudry told me very gently that the scaffolding *was* down, and I broke. I hadn't known how tightly I was holding on to the hope that someday I would look normal. When he took it from me I fell to pieces at his feet.

Ungrateful girl. Here's Dora per any doctor looking at me now: it ain't pretty, but it works. My take is that it really, *really* ain't pretty and it *kind* of works, but I have to keep that to myself. My parents brought me up to be brave and grateful, period. Each time I look in the mirror I am to rejoice at my good fortune in being alive. But being the lesser person that I am, all I feel when I look in the mirror is bitter disappointment followed by guilt.

Yes, I do know how much worse it could be, and reciting my function inventory to Jon triggered a wave of that old shame. I have friends, a career, and five working senses – to varying degrees, but I shouldn't be picky. We've all seen before-and-after images of face transplant recipients, and the difference between their situations and mine is obvious. Most of them are shut-ins on disability, many are blind in both eyes, and almost none can smell, eat or talk properly. Robbed of the faces they grew up with, they grapple daily with a radically altered sense of identity.

So why am I not better adjusted than I am, having known only successive versions of Dora? God knows I owe it to Grace to keep trying to accept what I have. No one worked harder than she did to help me develop a sense of self-esteem that didn't depend on how the world reacted to my looks. Unfortunately it was Grace against the world on that one, and I let the world win. Perhaps the donation was her way of admitting defeat.

I sit on the lid of the toilet hugging my knees. There are a number of factors I need to consider before I make my final decision, all of them more immediate than this *why* question. Yet my need to know what Grace was thinking persists and grows larger by the hour, crowding out everything else. Only Grace knew her real reasons for doing this and doesn't seem to have left me any clues. Jon hinted that perhaps it shouldn't matter, but it does. I can't go another step further until I figure it out.

Once she got over the shock of learning that I had applied for the list, Grace made it clear that she would respect any honest choice I made, but she never wavered in her conviction that a new face was not my answer. So how did she go from barely tolerating the idea to making it possible in the most personal way? It isn't just a matter of relenting; Grace's offer amounts to a full-out capitulation. It's tantamount to her admitting that she was wrong about how much my face mattered to my future happiness. Somewhere along the line she must have conceded the awful truth: that someone who looked like me would never be awarded the same share as someone who looked like her. To Grace, who abhorred injustice, that idea would have been intolerable.

This seems possible, even likely, but it doesn't make me feel better. It crushes me to think that Grace herself might have stopped believing. It was only because of Grace that I had any faith in the first place. I was always afraid she might be wrong about people being able to look past my appearance, but I desperately hoped she was right. The world she wanted me to believe I owned a place in was so much better than the one I was afraid might be real. Now I feel like a novitiate being handed a rifle by Mother Superior: forget all the idealism, it's turned out that love is not the answer after all. The true world is shallow and ruthless, and only the most radical of alterations will allow me to belong to it. As I am now, I am simply too much of a freak.

I am afraid that this might be what Grace's offer says about the world. I am terrified of what it says about me.

This little room is too bright, its surfaces too reflective. I close my eyes against the acid light but still see white porcelain, halls of it. And rubber gurney wheels, clicking smoothly across the miles of tile on their way to the remains of a life. Somewhere not far from here Grace's machine-run body waits, still warm from the morning sun.

I kneel and vomit, finally, nothing but foamy yellow bile. My throat is burning. I lie down with my cheek on the cool floor, palms flat against it to keep my body from sliding into the abyss. My watch says nineteen hours to yes or no.

* * *

Grace's first given name was Fortunata, intended as both a tribute and a blessing. Fortunata! Almost immediately my parents realized that the middle name they had chosen was much more appropriate. Grace was compact, elegant but portable, evocative but not unwieldy. They relieved her of the weight of Fortunata as a form of address but kept it on her papers so that it could still bring her luck.

Perhaps because of my mother's if-onlys I wondered a lot about luck as a kid, and causality in general. Luck was tricky because I never knew from what angle it should be viewed. My parents' friends said I was terribly unfortunate to have suffered the dog attack, but a dozen doctors had told me I was very lucky to have survived the blood loss. Who was right?

When I was about eight, my mother, who practiced Christianity on a handy as-needed basis, told me that God caused my suffering in order to test me. God tested people in all kinds of ways, she said. Even good things could be tests. A lottery win could be a test to see if the person was truly generous. A promotion at work might be a test of how someone used power. Even beauty, she said darkly, was a test of a person's vanity.

So what, I had to ask, might God be testing me for?

"Really He's testing both of us," Mother said. "God has given you this challenge to see whether or not you've got good character."

"What's good character?"

"Good character is when you've got your priorities straight." She laid a pious hand on her collarbone and looked heavenward. "And He gave me a disfigured daughter to test my strength. Lord knows I've done my best, Hellie. Most mothers wouldn't have held up half as well."

Here I missed my cue. I was supposed to have climbed onto her lap and kissed her, showered her with thanks for her selflessness. Instead I stood there frowning, scratching a mosquito bite on the back of my hand while I thought. In addition to my appearance and bookishness it was gaffes like this that made it difficult for my mother to like me.

"But what about Grace?" I asked. "Grace is pretty. Is God testing you with Grace too?"

"Oh ho. He certainly is." She said this with her heavy-lidded look, the one that meant *you have no idea.* "Parents can be tempted to love their beautiful child the most. They can be tempted to let the beautiful child do whatever she pleases, and never say no to her."

"They can?"

"Yes, ma'am. But do I love Grace more than the rest of you? Am I tempted to let her do whatever she pleases? Ask me, Hellie."

How odd. But, dutifully, I asked. "Are you tempted?"

"No, I am not," my mother said, with a depth of conviction that chilled me. "Not even a little."

It sounded serious, this test business. Mother seemed to have hers well in hand, but how in the world would I ever pass mine?

Bear up, Mother said. Be grateful. Don't complain. My burden entitled me to nothing, and that was what I should expect. No special treatment, no extra help, no sympathy. My face was my cross to bear, and I must understand why no one else wanted to bear it. "Most importantly," she said, "do not worship beauty. That way lies misery, Hellie."

I blinked. "I don't worship beauty."

She smiled, a strange curling of the lip. "No? Then stop following that sister of yours around like a lame little dog."

If my mother was right, God was testing us constantly. And I was going to fail in His eyes because I did love Grace more than my other sisters, and happily said yes to her all the time. Not because she was beautiful, but because she was my champion. Lord only knew how I was doing on the character problem, given that I wasn't even sure what priorities were.

Unsettled, I went to get Grace's take on the matter and found her lying on the sofa with a box of markers on her stomach, colouring on her cast. She was in an awful mood that week because she'd broken her wrist playing soccer and was missing a team trip to New York. There was no real reason why she couldn't have gone anyway, but I supposed Mother was demonstrating to God just how good she was at saying no to her beautiful child.

Grace declared the notion of the Divine character test to be utter bullshit. "God didn't mess up your face, Dog did. Cripes, you're eight years old. What kind of priorities are you supposed to have?"

"So you think I'm okay?" I asked hopefully. "I'm not in trouble?"

Grace groaned. "No, idiot, you're fine. Forget whatever she said. Hellie, you have to learn to ignore Mom when she says this crap. If she loves God so damn much she shouldn't go around blaming Him for stuff."

"Then do you think I'm unlucky?" It had struck me that, unlike Grace, I had no lucky element to my name, or anywhere. I didn't even own a rabbit's foot. Wasn't it foolish to be going through life without any sort of talisman?

"Luck, schmuck," Grace said. "You want to know my philosophy?" She stuck her gypsum-swathed wrist in my face.

Across the cast in elaborate two-inch-high red letters she'd written SHIT HAPPENS.

I never told Grace about the rest of that talk with my mother; it was too troubling. I was old enough at the time to be aware of the strange pride Mother took in how she treated my sister, and it ate at me. From my angle it looked a lot like Grace was being punished for turning out beautiful, which made no sense at all.

What my mother displayed in that conversation – vanity, resentment, distinct shades of jealousy and bitterness – took me years to understand. How it must have galled her, the closeness between Grace and me! We should have belonged to her, not each other. Grace was supposed to allow herself to be polished and exhibited, her mother's trophy; I ought to have fawned at her feet, symbol of her strength and compassion. But we shared a forceful instinct to resist her, and so became unending sources of disappointment. Only the twins were her true daughters, by turns simpering and hostile towards Grace and me, showing interest in us only as far as the world did. I never had the sense that they really knew either of us.

As we grew older I began to see with increasing clarity the continuum of beauty, and my place on it at the opposite end from Grace. Perhaps that formed part of our bond. In its own way, Grace's appearance was just as anomalous as mine. By the time she was in her early teens her beauty could not be ignored any more easily than Dora, which was almost certainly why she refused to discuss anything related to her looks. Grace wanted to be seen as Grace, and nothing infuriated her more than the way in which her emerging beauty seemed to be rendering her nameless to the world. Everywhere she went she had to assert that she was a person, not a prop. More and more often she was meeting people who wanted to use her, to place and admire her, but weren't terribly interested in who she was. Her only defense was to ignore the attention and the assumptions and keep being full-on Grace. She never said so, but I think it must have hurt that even her own mother couldn't see past her looks.

God's tests. It was my first inkling of how complicated a subject beauty was, especially among women. Especially among family.

Where at fourteen Grace had had very little use for mirrors, at the same age Bianca and Diana looked for them everywhere. Every surface, every image and reaction provided a reflection of some kind. Until recently Grace had irritated the twins with her devotion to outdoor sports and indifference to fashion, but now they appreciated her as a significant social asset. Where Grace was boys were, more than enough to go around. Suddenly the twins could not bear to be apart from their beloved older sister. Younger sisters, on the other hand, were a social liability. I was instructed not to make direct contact with the twins in public lest I did irreparable harm to their collective image.

That summer was Grace's sixteenth and her second as a lifeguard at the community pool. At sixteen Grace was practically a woman already, having to shave her armpits daily and squeeze her burgeoning curves into a no-nonsense regulation navy-blue swimsuit. The people who ran the rec programs loved her, so Mother insisted that she use her influence to get the twins jobs at the pool concession stand. Diana and Bianca begged her to say yes, and finally she agreed to recommend them only if they swore they wouldn't embarrass her.

At the pool Grace attracted – and ignored – a lot of attention. Still mostly flat-chested and narrow-hipped, the twins were desperate for the same kind of interest and found Grace's rejection of it hard to stomach. Diana in particular thought Grace was an idiot. Whenever Grace mentioned having to discourage a man's advances Diana would mutter darkly about "the waste." Grace finally asked what waste, exactly.

"Of opportunity," Diana said. Bianca nodded.

"Let me get this straight," Grace said. "You're criticizing me for passing up a date with a guy three times my age."

"With three times Daddy's salary," Diana said.

"That's a lot of good shoes," Bianca said.

"Jesus." Grace surveyed the two of them. "You're fourteen and you think this way."

"You're sixteen and you don't," Diana said. "Now *that's* hard to believe."

Grace walked away shaking her head.

"Pisses me off," Diana said to me later. "What I could do with her equipment."

Ah, but they had their own strange beauty. Even at fourteen, with their near-straight waists and too-big front teeth, the twins were entrancing. Bianca was prettier and rounder, Diana thinner and more graceful, but as fawn-legged fraternal complements they were an arresting pair and they knew it. They were in their new-found element at the pool that summer, taking turns preening behind the concession counter and tanning on the deck. They didn't distinguish themselves as particularly hard workers, but they showed up on time and got things done and by the end of the season people had begun to refer to "the Hallett girls" in a different tone altogether.

But of course I didn't count. I was the ten-year-old anti-beauty the others were forced to bring along, painfully skinny and pale, always having a terrible time keeping my hand-me-down swimsuit bottoms up. Because of my loose suit and the pool rules about long hair having to be tied back in the water, I almost never swam. Instead I lay on my towel in a corner on the concrete and read Madeleine L'Engle and watched my oldest sister pacing the deck or minding the swimmers from atop her guard tower, high and keen as a hawk.

Why wouldn't everyone look at Grace? She was lithe and strong and she had the bones of a hero. She wasn't a model type; she was too humanly proportioned, too *juicy*, and altogether far more appealing. She wore a ball cap over her ponytail and sunblock on her nose and lips and the tops of her ears, and her hair and freckled skin glowed like tiger's eye. I watched her, the boys watched her, the boys' fathers watched her, even the boys' mothers watched her although they tried very hard to look as if they were watching their kids or talking to their friends. If Grace was aware of any of this she showed no sign of it. She was there to guard lives and nothing would distract her from guarding them to the best of her ability. That was Grace.

I never swam unless the pool was nearly empty, which happened on only a few of the colder mornings. But there was an August day so hot that the heat rising from the black-painted concrete around the pool made everything beyond it shimmer into mirage. I lay sprawled on my towel for a long time, flattened by the weight of the air. Finally I got up, shoved my feet into my flip-flops and dragged myself over to the bottom of the guard tower. Grace was sucking on a juice box, her eyes glued to the water. She spoke to me without looking down.

"'Sup, Hellie? Where's your hat?"

"I got a question."

"You can ask questions with a hat on."

"Yeah, it's in my bag. But listen, Grace, I want to go swimming."

"So go."

"But my hair," I said, and then I had to wait while she blew her whistle on some horseplay.

"You have to tie your hair back or wear a bathing cap," she said when she was done. "I can lend you a cap if you want."

"Gracie," I said, but she shook her head.

"Nope, Hellie, sorry. Can't make an exception for you. But look, it'll be fine. Everybody's doing their thing. Nobody's looking at you."

"I don't want to scare the little kids," I said. That was my nightmare: frightening one four-year-old enough to kick off a whole chorus of shallow-end screaming.

"So stay in the deep end." Grace lifted her sunglasses and looked down at me. "Look, I'm right here if there's a problem. Just do your thing. You've got as much right as anybody to use the pool, so if you want to swim, swim. If somebody's got an issue with that, what's your attitude?"

"Screw 'em," I said, not very gamely.

"Bingo! And if they get scared, you go like this: *buk-buk-buk-buckaw!*" And she let out a chicken-screech that made a passing guard laugh and slap one of the guard tower posts.

I went back to my towel and sat there until I couldn't take it anymore, and then I found an elastic in my bag and knotted my hair into a loose ponytail that I could keep over the one side of my face as I got into the pool. I had thought I'd swim closer to where Diana and Bianca were wading around with some boys, but one look thrown my way from Diana reminded me that I wouldn't be welcome. Instead I slipped in near the wall where the water reached my ribcage and stood, delighting in the feel of my cooling belly and legs. I looked up at the guard tower where Grace was sitting with one leg tucked up underneath her, her face in shadow under the brim of her cap. She flashed me a grin and a big thumbs-up and I thumbs-upped her back, relieved that she had spotted me in the pool.

She was right. Everyone was doing their thing and nobody was looking at me, and after a few minutes of wall-hugging I threw caution to the hot August wind and lay back in the water. I don't know how long I floated face-up like that, eyes closed, before I felt shadows fall across my face.

I opened my eyes to a group of teenaged boys standing at the pool's edge, leaning over me. They yanked themselves backwards as if they had thought I was dead. I pulled myself up to standing and they stepped in again.

"What the *fuck*," one of them said wonderingly. Scruffy blond, familiar.

"Damn," said another boy, peering into my face. "Do both eyes work? I thought for sure that one wouldn't." This, I supposed, because of the scars around the socket.

"Are those worms?" The third boy pointed at my eyeball. His finger must have stopped quite close to my eye, because his fingertip disappeared from my field of view. All I could see was brown hand, brown arm, tanned shoulder, fascinated expression.

"Scars," I said.

Again, the simultaneous jerk backwards. "It talks," the blond one said.

"It can say *scars*," said the middle boy, "but its mouth is pretty messed up."

"Mouth?" The boy on the end had pulled his hand back and was pointing from a safer distance at another part of my face. "Cheek, man. Looks like a skull. Forehead, ear, nose – God, the nose is – and what's with the big dent there?"

None of this was directed to me. The boys didn't seem to regard me as self-aware; I might as well have been some interesting roadkill or a two-headed frog. I decided to say no more and wait it out. They would stare and comment until they got bored, and then they would go away.

Except that these boys weren't giving up as quickly as I'd hoped. They squatted on the edge of the pool and kept pointing, their fingers getting closer to my face. There was a ladder behind me, but one of the boys clambered over it and sat on the top step. The two boys at the pool's edge slipped into the water and waded up close. They were grinning like a pair of hyenas.

"It thinks it's going somewhere," one of them said.

"It's wrong," said the other.

I clamped my hand firmly on the waistband of my swimsuit bottoms and looked up at Grace's guard tower, praying that she was turned my way. She wasn't there. On the opposite side of the pool I could see Kevin, the head lifeguard, in the other guard chair, but Grace's seat was empty. I couldn't see her anywhere on the deck, but over on the far side of the pool Diana and Bianca were standing at the edge, shading their eyes and looking over in my direction. The twins! They would hurry over as soon as they figured out that I was in trouble.

They waved – finally! – and I lifted my hand in response. So did the boys.

"Call them over," one of them said.

"Nah, don't," said the blond boy. "They won't like it."

What? And then it struck me where I'd seen him before: wading around with the twins.

"Think they can see her from there?"

Diana and Bianca were frozen in their far-gaze attitudes, staring over at us. "Oh, yeah," said one of the boys. "They can see her."

I dropped my eyes. Down through the water the light was swinging in white ellipses across my legs and feet. Where was Grace? And why weren't the twins coming over? I wanted to call out to them but the boys were pressing in close and my voice was trapped in my throat like a bird struggling to take flight.

The blond boy pushed his face into mine. "Heads up, *freak*."

"Wig!" shouted a voice from behind me. Then someone grabbed my ponytail and pulled sharply, dragging me back and down by the crown of my head. I went under the water, unable to see through a miasma of bloodshot crimson. When I struggled to rise a hand smacked me in the chest and pushed me back down. I twisted, panicking. Which way was up? Water filled my nose, ran for the hollows behind my eyes and cheeks. I wondered briefly about drowning and then remembered that my sister was a lifeguard here. Better not drown on Grace's shift or she'd kill me.

Strong hands under my shoulder blades, lifting me up. I broke the surface to find Kevin in the water with me, supporting me by my back and neck. Grace was looking down at us from the pool deck. Somehow the forces of good had been mobilized during the few seconds I'd been under, which was both a relief and a terrible embarrassment. I'd had a good ducking but was otherwise fine. I told this to the dark shape of Kevin's face above me before he had a chance to ask.

"Hear that?" he said to Grace, who was leaned over the edge of the pool, toes gripping the concrete. "A-OK." Grace pulled me up onto the ladder. Kevin hoisted himself onto the deck and sat beside me, shedding bright droplets from his brown skin like an otter while I sneezed out about a gallon of chlorinated water. "Hey, where're you going?" he said to the boys, who had gotten out of the water and were easing off in the direction of the change rooms. "C'mon back. All the way back. That's it."

Grace put my towel around my shoulders. "Goddammit, Hellie," she said. "I was gone for five minutes. Kid with a nosebleed. I'm so sorry."

"I'm all right," I said. "It was nothing."

"Nothing bullshit." She was holding my face, checking for damage. "Sure you're okay?"

I nodded and wiped my nose with the corner of my towel. In truth my scalp ached and my sinuses felt like they'd been thoroughly reamed, but I kept that to myself.

Grace got to her feet and stood in front of the boys. Kevin got up and stood behind her.

"You are all going to Hell," she said. Calm but very definite, like she'd put it on the schedule herself.

"Howzat?" the blond boy said.

"You fucked with my sister," Grace said. "Therefore you go to Hell. Maybe not now, but someday."

"Grace," Kevin said, with a little smile.

The boys had been smirking, elbowing one another, goggling at Grace's breasts. Suddenly they looked a lot less comfortable.

"*That's* your sister?" one of them asked, indicating me with a jerk of his head. "Like, adopted, right?"

"Look, we thought she was sick," the blond boy said. "We didn't know she was your sister. We thought some kid with, like, flesh-eating disease was in the pool. 'Scuse us for being concerned."

"Oh, I see," Grace said. "You were abusing her for the greater good."

Here I had to speak up, because it always bothered me when people got their biology facts wrong. "If I had necrotizing fasciitis I wouldn't be at the pool," I said. "I'd be in the hospital."

"There you go," Kevin said. "Perfectly healthy."

"Well, holy shit, *look* at her," the blond boy said, throwing a hand in my direction. "That ain't *normal*."

"We're done here," Kevin said. He told the boys to get their stuff and leave the pool. As of that moment they were out, banned for the summer, and lucky it wasn't worse.

We watched as they slouched out through the gate barefoot, holding their shoes and towels in bundles against their skinny abdomens. On the other side of the chain-link fence I saw Diana and Bianca run to catch up with them. I looked up at Grace, who had just returned to her seat on the guard tower. Even from where I stood I could tell from her narrowed eyes and tight mouth that she had seen the twins, too.

After supper that night Grace followed Diana and Bianca up to their room and the yelling commenced. I couldn't hear much of the twins, just Grace repeating her favourite word: *bullshit, bullshit, total bullshit and you both know it.* I was trying to finish *A Wind in the Door* and had to go outside to the hammock to concentrate on the last chapter.

It was almost too dark out to read when Grace came out from the house. When I saw her I braced for the usual roughhousing. Grace liked to tackle me in the hammock and push my face into her sweaty armpit, yelling *how's your nose working today, Hellie?* But this time she didn't. Instead she took my book away and lay down with me, wrapping her arms firmly around me.

"Hellie-Bellie," she said. "Were you scared today?"

"A little."

"'Course. How you doing now?"

"I'm all right."

"Yeah," she said. "You coped with that shit way better than I did."

I wasn't sure about that. It wasn't the first time I'd been teased or insulted in public, but no one had ever put their hands on me like that before and I hated to admit just how frightened I had been. Up until then I had been protected from that degree of negative attention, or rescued long before it went anywhere. My scalp was still aching, but pain was nothing new. It was *freak* that would not leave me alone, and the expressions on the boys' faces. What was I to do with such naked horror and disgust?

But Grace seemed to think I was dealing with it, so I had to make like I was. "Bunch of idiots," I said. "Flesh-eating disease. Morons."

"You recognize that kid?"

"The twins like him."

"Stevie Wilhelm." Grace made a bad-smell face. "Diana's crush. Can't stand that little weasel. She and Bianca have been hanging out with the whole weaselly group of them all summer. FYI, the twins are pretty pissed at Kevin and me right now for kicking their douchebag boyfriends out. If either of them says one damn thing to you, Hellie, you tell them to eat shit and die."

"Grace!" I giggled fearfully, imagining Diana's expression. "I can't say that!"

"Oh, yes, you can. Tell them I said so. That was anti-social, dangerous behaviour. Crap like that does not go down on my watch, especially to my sister."

I thought about Diana and Bianca and those boys: how they were with me, and how completely different they were with each other – the twins simpering and coquettish, the boys slow-smiling and exchanging knowing looks. Like a dance, a closed ritual. It wasn't just that I was younger; whatever the twins were to the boys, I wasn't even considered to be a member of the same species.

"Diana and Bianca didn't come over," I said. "They saw me, but they didn't come." This had been bothering me more than I thought it should. Evidently it also bothered Grace.

"I gave them shit for that," she said. "But *I* should have been there first. I should have gotten Kev to deal with the nosebleed. I only went because I was right there and I thought I'd just be a sec."

"That's your job," I said.

"Yeah, but I should have sent Kev." She gave me a little squeeze. "He couldn't see that you were in trouble until things got rough. No offense to him, but I would have picked up on it way earlier." She would have, too. "I'm really sorry, Hellie. I didn't think anyone would treat you like that at my pool."

"It's okay, Grace."

"No, it's not. You must have thought I abandoned you."

"No," I said. "Never."

Grace was quiet for a long time, resting her chin on the top of my head. Above us the last of the light had ebbed away and I couldn't tell leaves from sky anymore. The bug zapper by the back door was getting busy with moth traffic. I lay curled against Grace and breathed.

I understood why Grace hadn't been on hand to rush to my rescue. What baffled me were the twins. Not that they were angry with Grace – that was hardly unusual – but that they had watched the boys with me and done nothing.

Grace had a weak spot for boys, but it wasn't like the twins. Grace was in love with life, addicted to the fullness that movement and food and sun and other bodies brought her senses. Her companions were all life-lovers like her, friendly doers interested in the company of anyone on board for the group adventure. Grace would never trade me away for any of them, and they would never require her to.

You don't show much, she said to me once. Especially when something hurts. She said it had nothing to do with my face; it was like I thought I had to swallow it all down. She couldn't always tell what I was thinking, and it worried her. Grace said that if I let my feelings out once in a while maybe I wouldn't get so many stomach aches.

"Gracie," I said into her sweatshirt.

"Hellie."

"Am I a freak?"

It was a silly question, a blatant solicitation of reassurance, and I wouldn't have put it to anyone but Grace. When she answered her tone was light, but underneath it she sounded anguished and weary and much older than sixteen.

"Helena Anne Hallett, you are so unfreaky it's not funny. You are the sanest, smartest, humanest human I know. You are so normal your name should be Norm. In fact, it's my pleasure to inform you that you've won an award for being so unfreakily, humanly normal. Congratulations. Please allow six to eight weeks delivery for your prize."

My "prize," which arrived in the mail exactly six weeks later, was a pretty little engraved name bracelet. "Let's see," Bianca said, and Diana grabbed my wrist. They peered at the script.

"We don't get it," Diana said. "Who's Norm?"

Sixteen hours to the answer I don't have.

I wish she had left a letter. That's the ridiculous thing I'm wanting now, sitting out on my balcony watching the sun go down on the first full day of my life without Grace.

Like most of its brethren, this hotel is a low-rise job with parking lots instead of landscaping, but it's at the end of town where the buildings trail off. By some miracle my balcony looks out over a farmer's field, one apparently lying fallow. It isn't exactly a view, but beyond it there's the Niagara Escarpment with a gap big enough to admit the sunset all the way to the horizon line. The cooling early summer air is good out here, tinged with the faint rotten sweetness of soil and manure. I wish to God that Grace had left me a letter telling me why she did this.

I should call Arthur and see if a note was left out of my envelope. Something that begins *Dear Hellie, if you're reading this I guess I'm dead and you're trying to work out the face thing. I know that it goes against everything I said before, so let me explain.*

When I lean back I can see Jon still sleeping, his body splayed out like an open hand. Jon is nothing if not open. He has a certain need to fling himself at things, push them in all directions to see what breaks when. It's an extremity that extends to his extremities, even in sleep. Over and over he reaches out, heedless of the boundaries of the bed.

Jon sat next to me in my first Biological Concepts of Health lecture on my first day of my first year of undergrad. He was noisy, restless, interested in everyone around him. He borrowed paper from me and complimented me on my penmanship. I saw the flicker of his expression when I pulled my hair back to keep it off my page and I wished he was sitting on my good side. Something always passes over people's faces when they first see me, but it isn't the same something with everyone. With Jon it was mildest surprise and it faded almost immediately. Throughout the lecture he studied my cheek and profile with subdued and friendly curiosity, as if admiring an intricate tattoo.

Like me, Jon was a child steeped in medicine. His father was a plastic surgeon who specialized in reconstructive work. Jon was born with a cleft palate, but Dr. Faulkner oversaw a repair so fine you'd never have known. He taught Jon to read x-rays and showed him before-and-after pictures of the many Cinderella stories he'd presided over. I wasn't the first patchwork person Jon had seen, although he maintains that I'm the most interesting. His dad did his best to steer him towards medical school and a surgery specialization, but like me Jon seemed to have been born knowing he was going to be a vet. Unlike me he never had to make a secret of it.

When we were picking up our books after that first lecture he told me that he was drafting me for his study group. He was collecting only the smartest kids, he said. He needed the help and we needed his panache.

I suppose it began there. Loving Jon is either my most ascetic practice or my greatest indulgence: I suffer in silence but refuse to give it up. He knows, and he knows it's the reason I sometimes say awful things to him, and it's the reason he lets me. There is no question that I would be or do or forgive anything for him, so it's only fair that I should be allowed to yell at him once in a while. Jon needs me and adores me, but I don't think I want to know how far it extends beyond that. I absolutely do not want to know what role Dora has played in maintaining the slight distance between us. Grace taught me never to ask a question unless I was prepared to hear the answer.

A groaning yawn inside: he's up. His mobile is buzzing. "Fuck," he says wearily. Then: "Hey, babe." I watch him pace in and out of my field of view, hair sticking up like it's been swiped with a giant tongue.

From his tone I know that the caller is Leanne. When he talks to her he always sounds like he's out on the farthest, thinnest edge of his patience, just as he has with all her predecessors. I can never figure out what he gets out of these relationships, other than the obvious. The women are all beautiful and demanding and trying in exactly the same ways, and when he talks about them he always sounds beleaguered and exhausted. Whenever I complain about his disappointingly mainstream taste in girlfriends he just shrugs. Doesn't even bother to defend himself, because he doesn't understand it either.

The kicker is that Jon is staggeringly, jaw-droppingly smart. That's not to say that he never does anything stupid, because the emotional component of his IQ doesn't reach quite as far into the stratosphere as the rest of it. But he has the kind of fast, flexible intelligence that shows itself in a thousand astonishing ways over the course of any given hour, and not one of these women has ever shown the slightest appreciation for it. It never changes: they fall for a tall, fit vet with an easy laugh, and then they complain endlessly about the hours he works.

He comes to the screen door scratching himself like an ape. He checks his phone one more time and clamshells it. "Hi from Leanne."

"As if, Faulkner."

He grins. "She bugs you, eh?"

"Probably not as much as she bugs you."

"Well, between your face and your brains you completely freak her out. So you win."

He leans in the doorway looking out at the pinkening sky, the room a well of shadows behind him. "Very pretty, Dora. Have you eaten?"

"No."

"Soup. I'll get room service. Anything else?"

"Can I borrow your car for a couple of hours?"

"If you eat something you can have my car. I mean it. I'll sign it over to you today."

"I'm going to go see Jason."

"Whatever, Hellie. It's your car."

After he calls down for food he comes out onto the balcony and takes the other chair. He pokes me with his toe.

"Where you at, Hallett?"

I shrug. "I'll have a better idea after I talk to Jason."

"Good idea, talking to him."

I look at him sideways. "You think so."

"Yes. I was going to suggest it."

"Why?"

He stretches out his legs. Stares at them. "Are you leaning towards yes?"

"I haven't decided."

"But you're considering it."

"I've thought about it for a long time, Jon. I told you that."

"But your sister's face, Hellie? Doesn't that change things a little?"

"Of course, but –"

"Because there's thinking and there's thinking." Now he's looking at me. "Sitting around dreaming about a new face doesn't count."

"I know that, Jon."

"Well, good. And it's about time Jason crossed your mind, because psychologically this could be even worse for him than for you."

"It wouldn't look the same on me," I say. "It never could, even if the transfer was absolutely perfect. My brain wouldn't move the muscles the same way she did."

"Beside the point."

"No, it's not. You're worried about Jason being screwed up by seeing Grace's face on me, and I'm telling you that I wouldn't look like her. There might be some resemblance around the nose, but that would be it. My bone structure and face shape are different. I probably still wouldn't be perfectly symmetrical."

"Then why do it? Why take the risk?"

He's leaning on me, reneging on his promise to stay neutral. I should be surprised that it didn't happen sooner.

"Grace would have cleared this with Jason, Jon. She wouldn't have just gone and done it without his permission. I'm still going to talk to him and find out how he really feels. But if he can look me in the eye and tell me he's okay with it, he's okay with it."

"And you're sure he'll be straight with you."

"Absolutely."

"And what about the kids?"

"We'll talk about them too."

Jon slides down lower in his chair. He looks gloomy and Churchillian, chin buried in his chest. "And what about you?"

The nausea is creeping back, pooling like oil in my stomach. "What about me?"

"You're saying that nothing about this idea weirds you out even a little?"

I remind him that I've had a lot of surgery, including bone and tissue grafts from donors. If I was ever troubled by the idea of my face being cut open or receiving parts from other people, I was forced to get over it a long time ago.

"Not that," he says. "The sister thing. The fact that it's Grace. You're avoiding thinking about that part of it, but there's no going back if it messes you up."

Beyond the light-pool of the hotel, bats are wheeling in the thickening dark. It's getting noisy now: dusk birdsong, cicadas, crickets. From somewhere beyond the field there's the deep rubber band twang of a bullfrog. Jon is frowning at his feet, mouth suppressed in a line. He wants to say more but is trying to be good.

"I don't have an answer for you," I tell him. "I could think about it for years and still not have any idea what it might be like. How can I know without going through it?"

"Well, what about the rest of your family? You going to factor them in?"

"This is between me and Grace."

"Oh, come *on*, Hellie. That's ridiculous. That's just wishful thinking, imagining that it's got nothing to do with them. You're seriously going to leave them out of it?"

"Yes," I say in a small voice.

"So you'd actually go ahead without talking to them, and your parents and sisters would just have to deal with it when they found out. And you know that they would find out." He's openly reproachful now, and angry. "Well, that is pretty damn selfish if you ask me. I wouldn't have pegged you for doing something like that. Oh, but –" He holds up his hand. "That's right, you *didn't* ask me. Sorry. Forgot that I'm supposed to keep my mouth shut except to agree."

"Jon." Tears are beginning to prick at the back of my throat. It smarts, being called selfish, especially by him. "You know my family. What do you think they'd say?"

"They'd probably say no, but that doesn't mean you shouldn't at least tell them it's going to happen. Warn them."

"They wouldn't care what I wanted, or what Grace was trying to do. They'd say no just to say no. My mother has this weird scheme of things, who deserves what –"

"Don't work yourself up. I get it."

"There's no time to talk to them properly about it." I am pleading, and it sounds so weak. "They don't have to know who the donor was. They'll just know it was someone's face and now it's mine. They don't know what it's like for me the way I am now, and they don't care. They'd fight me. If I told them in advance, they'd do everything they could to stop it from going forward. You know they would."

I hunch over in my chair, wrapping my arms around the oily ball in my stomach. The only thing uglier than Dora is Dora crying, and I'd rather choke to my death on tears than subject either of us to that mess yet again.

Jon sounds so weary now. "Hellie, I just need to know that you've looked at this from every angle. It's huge. It could cause a permanent rift between you and your family, and what if you need them down the road? What if the whole thing goes sour? If you're going to go ahead, you'd better be ready for the worst."

I squeeze my midsection, trying to make the ball smaller. "What do you want me to say? How many problems can I solve in the amount of time I have to do this? Not very damn many."

"No." He sighs. "Not many. Stinks that it has to be this way." He shakes his head. "You must really want this."

I don't answer. How do I explain to someone so beautifully normal what it's like for me? Especially to Jon, who, bless him, has never seen anything horrifying in my appearance?

"So call the lawyer," Jon says. "Call him right now. Tell him it's a conditional yes and you'll confirm as soon as you speak with Jason." He doesn't say it out loud but I can hear the last phrase clearly: *I dare you.*

He waits, then pokes me with his toe again. "Well? How about it?"

"Stop." I pull my leg away. "I'm not calling him now, Jon. It's after nine."

"Any time day or night, he said."

"You want me to rush into this."

"I want to know why you won't call him now, if you're planning to do it."

"I have to speak to Jason."

"Meaning you have reservations. And you still want to know why she did it."

"Yes, Faulkner, I do. And so what."

He throws out his hands. "And so what *difference* does it make? It's *your* decision. It doesn't matter what Grace was thinking. It's like you're sitting here still waiting for her to tell you what to do! But *I'm* the one who gets bitched out for being prescriptive."

"I'm not bitching you out."

"What do you plan to do if you find out that Grace was hoping you'd say no?"

"She wasn't. Grace wouldn't play games like that."

"And what if Jason says no, huh?"

"Then I won't do it."

"No matter how badly you want it."

I feel like kicking him.

"Here's that advice you don't want," he says. "Whether you go ahead or not, make sure you understand why."

"I'll be damned if I let my family stop me, Jon."

"Fair enough. But don't you dare go ahead as a fuck-you to your mother, either."

I glare at him, full-on basilisk. He ignores it. "And for Christ's sake, take a minute to think about what you would lose. You have a face, Hellie. A working face that the people in your life might actually have some affection for. Please, please promise me you'll think about that. Think about us."

But I have thought about you, and others, my whole thinking life. Tried to spare you from the sight of my makeshift face, from the burden of association with a freak, from the necessity of pretending she doesn't matter. Affection for Dora? Live behind her, my love, and then tell me how much affection you have left.

Still, it's Jon who is asking me for this. If it was anyone else I wouldn't deign to answer.

"If I promise," I say between my teeth, "will you get off my back?"

"Hell, no," Jon says. "This is way too big for that."

He reaches for my hand. "You're not selfish, okay? I only want this to be good for you." He sighs. "I just don't know how you can possibly make a rational decision about this right now. You haven't even begun to grieve yet."

I am silent, swallowing tears. We look out into the flickering, singing dark for a long time before he squeezes my fingers and lets them go.

Jon is in the shower when room service knocks. I open the door for the cart and sign the receipt. It's only when I half-smile at the attendant as I'm giving him his tip that he gets a good look at me. He steps back, then reaches for the bills. As he wishes me a very good evening I watch a red flush creeping up his neck like frost.

That. I stare at the door the man has closed behind him. I wish Jon had seen it. That look is what I want to bring an end to. Forget my family, forget Jason and the girls, forget Jon: right now I believe I'd trade every last thing away for the promise of never being looked at like that again.

*/) */) */)

Consider the face.

Functionally: ports and surfaces for sensory input (taste, smell, sight, touch, all in close proximity to hearing); intake/output points for breath, fluid and food, with built-in barrier/filter systems; expression-board for the display or transmission of emotional states and signals; delivery mechanism for the articulation and amplification of spoken communications. And that's just the moving parts.

We cull a great deal of information from a face before it moves a single muscle. Approximate age, sun exposure, time spent worrying, smiling or smoking. Clues to general health: pallor, ruddiness, the flush of fever? Bloodshot eyes, dark circles, lips cracked or soft? Acne, rosacea, a fine web of drinker's veins? Then there are the genes expressed through the facial features, much more specific and readily identifiable than height or body type. For starters there's skin, hair and eye colour. Epicanthal folds, flared nostrils, eyebrows that arch or grow wild. Dimples, double chins, widow's peaks and bow lips. Whose nose, whose eyes, whose lantern jaw? Family resemblances matter.

One of the many painful aspects of extensive facial trauma, especially when suffered very young, is the destruction of this inheritance. Then it is all a guess, all hypothetical. I always thought, though I was never sure, that I would have had a neat, narrow nose like my mother's. I thought that if my smile were symmetrical it would be a lot like Daddy's. Instead I was left with a unique arrangement of nasal cartilage and a one-sided grin that was to be mine alone. Nor would any child of mine ever look like me; at most they would be my might-have-been. Any part of them not obviously taken from their father's side would make me wonder if it could have been mine, had my face developed normally.

But beyond function, beyond indications of fitness and emotional state and genetic makeup, there is the matter of aesthetics. It's less arbitrary than most of us would like to think. Ask a psychologist, biologist or cognitive scientist and you'll learn that many of the aesthetic preferences we imagine are unique to each of us are in fact hard-wired into the board of virtually every member of our species. We like symmetry because it indicates normal development and helps with easy identification of our conspecifics. We prefer facial proportions that are linked to optimal function. We take particular notice of individuals with chest-waist-hip ratios that signal fertility or strength. It's all about choosing with whom to reproduce and share resources, and our ancient brains make one snap judgment after another without us having a clue.

Because I know this, I forgive people the looks that cross their faces when they first see me. Their wiring is telling them *wrong! Broken, diseased! Stay away!* Talking to the wiring – saying *she's fine, everything works, she's not a monster* – is like reasoning with a screaming child: it doesn't end the reaction. Try as it might, the prefrontal cortex can't rationalize away the old warnings. You might quiet the child, but the fear is still there.

But a face like Grace's that satisfies the ancient brain has unparalleled value. It is a commodity on which both the bearer and those around her can trade. Diana and Bianca had a fraction of Grace's aesthetic capital but they worked overtime to make the most of it. Listening to their obsessions over where God had chosen to place their noses and lips versus where He might have placed them had He been feeling even slightly more magnanimous, I had to wonder whether it might be harder to be almost something than not even close to it.

In one strange way, I can more readily imagine what it's like to be shockingly beautiful than to be a person of average appearance. Everywhere that Grace went, no matter how much she played down her looks, people stared. When strangers commented on her beauty they were as open and loud and indifferent to her feelings as when they remarked on my disfigurement. This is why I've never craved that kind of beauty for myself. I'm happy to enjoy it in other people, but because of Grace I always understood that it came with its own set of complications. All I ever wanted was a normal, unremarkable face and whatever came with it. Given the chance, all I would ask for is that which would have been mine.

Funnily enough, it was Diana who first taught me about symmetry and classical proportions. I always thought that if she'd been more inclined to study she would have made a fine anthropologist. You couldn't ignore biological imperatives, she said. I was getting ready for my first high-school party and she had taken it upon herself to prepare me for the possibility that no boy would ask me to dance.

"It's not exactly that you're ugly, Hellie," she said, as kindly as she could. "It's just that your face looks really, really wrong."

It must be said that the boys at the science-centric high school I attended generally found it hard to ask any girl to dance. They were a better bunch than my middle-school classmates, but unfortunately Dora's cryptic versions of standard facial expressions tended to compound everyone's preexisting adolescent awkwardness. I wasn't asked out on dates, but I wasn't tortured, either, and there was something to be said for that. In the meantime there were more surgeries and the school part of school to contend with, and I had my own reasons for wanting to excel.

Grace helped me hash out my covert plans for veterinary college when I had just turned fourteen. Even then it was obvious that I was headed towards the biological sciences, but my sister agreed that revealing my chosen career to my parents too soon would be disastrous.

"They'll freak," Gracie said. "You mention the v-word and they will utterly lose their shit. They'll say you've got some weird victim-sympathizing-with-attacker thing going on. Unless you want the grief I wouldn't bring it up. Not yet, anyway."

She'd just gotten home from university for the summer and we were lying on foam mats beside the pool at her boyfriend Jason's house. Because of my skin grafts I had to wear gallons of sunblock, so as usual Grace was turning a lovely burnished caramel and I was not. I asked her when she thought I should bring it up.

"When it's absolutely too late for them to stop you." Grace rolled onto her back and drew one knee up. The skin above her hips was even darker than the rest of her belly, a mystery.

"I'm on your side, Hellie, but you have to look at it from their point of view. They almost lost you. Daddy's never gotten over it." She squinted at me, shading her eyes with her hand. I liked the way they matched the Aegean blue backdrop of the pool behind her. "It's cool how you love animals like you do. I think it's amazing, but Mother and Daddy don't get it."

I shrugged. It seemed to me that I'd been born with an affinity for animals so strong that it would take a far greater force than that dog's bite to dislodge it. If anything, his distress had fed my desire to reach out to all others like him. I was the sole daughter who could not accept the household ban on dogs, who begged every Christmas and birthday for a puppy, who as a child threw tantrums when I was not allowed to pet dogs on the street. To mollify me there had been surprise gifts of lizards, turtles, tropical fish (frequently replaced) and even a budgie, but nothing with real teeth and especially no dogs. Never were there to be dogs. And I, who dreamed of being a vet and ached for my own companion animals, felt terribly deprived.

My father, who had long ago forgotten what it was like to look upon me without being wracked by guilt, had told me I must stop asking. In tears he had begged me to make an outlandish wish so that he could satisfy it: "Anything else, Helena. I mean it. Absolutely anything but a dog."

I didn't want anything else, but I didn't want to see him like that, either. I stopped asking, but still I yearned for my dog. If I had to wait for my parents' permission to associate with dogs (or even cats!) I'd be well past retirement age before I had my own.

But at the moment Grace was home with me, the June sky was infinite and no problem was insoluble. Jason brought us

Cokes from the house and flopped down on the deck alongside Grace. They were in the same Phys.Ed program at school and I liked him a lot. He had earned big points with Grace by inviting me over to swim with them any time I liked, the only boyfriend of any of my sisters who was genuinely willing to include me in anything. Whenever we showed up he was skimming the pool for us, his wiry brown body arcing over the water to reach leaves and waterlogged wasps. Jason wore electric yellow surf shorts and sculpted his white-blond hair into arrow-shaped crests that made him seem always angled forward, ready to cut a swath through any situation. Grace said that he was unusual because he was goal oriented but super mellow. My other sisters called him a flake, my parents said he probably smoked a lot of pot, and I decided immediately that Grace could marry him if she liked. He was perfect.

After he lay down with us they talked about school. Jason was happy in the Phys.Ed program; he would graduate and then see what the universe delivered. Grace was less happy, but not clear on why. Her roommate, Katie, was an English major, and all that poetry she had lying around was doing something to Grace. As she'd begun to absorb it, some indefinable yearning had taken hold, but she had no idea what it was or what to do with it. The notion of changing majors was laughable.

"You're the smart one, Hellie. I just wanted to be outside running around. But the stuff Katie's reading…we didn't do that in high school. If we had, I might have tried harder in class."

She snapped her fingers. "Got it. Tell them you want to be a doctor. Go through for all the biomedical stuff, write your MCATs, and then you break it to them. That'll be about eight years from now." She smiled a gorgeous, juicy smile, hugely pleased with herself. "Who says I'm just a dumb jock?"

"She's right, Cookie," Jason said, stretching his arms over his head. At fourteen I twisted up with happiness whenever

Jason called me Cookie or Bunny or 'Lena; I'd never had sweet nicknames from a boy before. "Good plan. It'll work."

Then Grace took advantage of Jason's elongation and rolled him into the pool, and then he pulled her in with him, and then they both got out and picked me up and swung me like a squealing hammock into the water and jumped in after me. So that was the end of that conversation.

Grace had embarked on two love affairs that year, both of which would endure to the day she died. The first, of course, was Jason. Then, through Katie's copy of *Leaves of Grass*, Grace met Walt Whitman and found her literary soulmate.

She and Walt were separated by a country and over a century but they saw the world through the same lens. His was the poetry Grace would have written if she been able to find words for her longing. The same love was there, the same desire and urgency and need to be present. Listen, his poems said to her. Feel all of a thing, taste all of it, observe, touch, absorb and remember. The beauty of the world had enveloped and broken and remade his heart just as it did to hers.

She never did change majors, and I didn't encourage her to. I had always thought of her as wise beyond her years, yet couldn't – or wouldn't – acknowledge her intellectual potential aloud. I was the smart one, just as she said. I would never have consciously denied Grace anything, but I am afraid that I withheld some words that might have made a difference if I had said them in time. I would never have admitted it then, but I wanted one thing to be mine alone.

* * *

I am sitting across from Jason at the table in his darkened kitchen, watching him make himself eat. He and the girls have promised one another that they'll try to get regular fuel and rest, so now he's listlessly dipping and stripping chicken wings. Millie and Georgia are asleep on the sofa in the next room, having suddenly found upstairs to be too far away from Daddy for comfort. Jason asks me to help him with the wings, but I shake my head.

"Right," he says. "I forgot about the chicken thing."

Like a number of us in small animal practice I've pretty much gone off boned chicken, especially wings. I find it reminds me to an unsettling degree of the anatomy of my patients.

He's not really eating them either, mostly just picking at shards of flesh on his plate. "This is stupid hard," he says. I nod.

"But you're trying too, right? You're not a big eater at the best of times."

"Faulkner fed me before I came over. Poured soup down my gullet."

"Good." He pinches a hand wipe out of its foil square. "You're in on the pact. Not good for the girls if all the family wheels fall off at once."

"Can I have one of those? I like the smell."

The cloth inside the foil packet is unnaturally cool. I run it over my wrists, the back of my neck. Jason opens another and does the same.

"I don't know what to tell you about the girls," he says. "I have no idea how I would explain it to them, because

I don't know what they can handle. I don't see myself telling them who the face came from. Not now, anyway. Maybe they'd figure it out down the road, but it's way too much for this age."

"You don't think it would mess them up, even later on?"

"I have no idea, Hellie. Things might be different for them. By the time they're old enough to understand this it could be pretty common, like the kidney thing is to us."

"But we don't identify people by their kidneys. I couldn't pick Grace's organs out of a lineup."

"What I mean is, it won't be a freaky new idea. It isn't that new now. Or maybe it will always be freaky. Who knows." He sighs. "But her kidneys are being donated, and her heart, liver, corneas – everything that's usable. That's what she wanted."

"But it's all waiting on me."

He shrugs.

"I don't think anyone expected you to make up your mind right away. I sure didn't." He pokes at a piece of chicken flesh with his index finger. "Anyway, you probably know more about this than the rest of us put together. Is it an all-or-nothing deal? Because if you don't like the idea of taking the whole face, maybe you could just use a part of it. Is that even possible?"

I nod. The truth is that partials work better if the damage is top or bottom – replacing the entire nose and mouth, for example. My problems are left-right, so if only the damaged area is replaced I'll still wind up looking asymmetrical. One advantage of a full transplant is that it's not patchwork. But I don't think I should go into this kind of detail with Jason, who has thus far kept it together remarkably well for a man contemplating the imminent carving-up of his beloved. Either he and Grace talked the donation through until he was at peace with the idea, or it simply isn't real to him yet.

"Jason, I have to ask you something but I don't know if you're allowed to answer."

He wipes his mouth. "Allowed by who? Arthur?"

"By Grace. Did she ever tell you what she hoped I'd decide?"

Where he finds a smile I can't know, but he does. "Hellie. You know Grace. She wasn't attached to an outcome. She wanted you to do whatever you wanted."

"That's it? She didn't say anything about why?"

He thinks, head cocked like a retriever. He's so blond that the small halo of light above the table is silvering his hair and eyebrows. Millie has that hair, holy-looking on a child.

"She knew you wanted a transplant," he says finally, "and she decided that she should let go of her own ideas about what was good for you. That's all she told me, and I really think that's all there was to it." He watches me for a moment. "You think something else?"

"I don't know what to think."

He spreads his hands. "We both see − saw − this body as a shell. Grace was adamant that she didn't want anybody getting sentimental about hers after she was gone. She said her parts should go to whoever could use them, and burn the rest. She didn't even want me keeping an urn. Just scatter her and let go."

But that was then, and what she wanted for herself. What about Jason, now? I am afraid to ask.

He feels my question anyway, and holds up his hand. There's a twist of jute around his wrist, two elastic bands, a sport watch. He used the watch as a timer for Grace and her laps.

"Please don't ask me how I feel about it," he says. "I don't know. I don't want to think about it. It was hers to offer you, so take it if you want it. I'll deal with it somehow. So will the girls. You were her sister; you would have looked like her anyway."

"But if you don't –"

He shakes his head. "I had my chance to say no."

We sit in silence for a while, listening to the tick of the refrigerator. "Of course," he says suddenly, "she didn't know. You write these things but you don't really believe anyone's ever going to have to read them. We did our wills because we thought we should, we had a kid already. Grace said that by the time she died she'd be so wrinkled it would all be a huge joke. They'd tell you and you'd say yech, thanks but no thanks. She didn't know."

He sits across from me looking like a very senior camp counselor, the farthest thing imaginable from a widower. Except for his eyes, the grieving depths of which are almost unreadable. I think I might have the same fathomless here-not-here gaze. We will have to go forward together like this, both blind, taking turns finding the way.

I return to the hotel in the darkest, smallest hours to find Jon still awake, awash in pale TV flicker. He's stayed up to tell me that he can't get his next shift covered and has to go first thing in the morning.

I lie down and he stretches out beside me, fitting himself against me like a second spine. Animal me would be delirious if she wasn't utterly exhausted. I think he asks me if I can sleep like this.

I can sleep. I can even dream. I am pushing my way through a wild thicket of images, moving low and sure. I am leonine, all muscle, and I have no enemies. I am wearing my sister's face and it has conferred her spirit upon me, making me brave.

⁂

By my final year of vet college I had a good tight core of friends, mostly from Jon's original batch of study group recruits. Those of us who had made the cut after undergrad kept the well-entrenched group study habit going and took care of one another. I watched as Jon took full advantage of the favourable female-to-male ratio, bouncing pinball-style across the months from one woman to the next until he got to Courtney. Then, unfortunately, he settled down.

Everything about Courtney was breathtaking. Hair, features, skin texture, bust-waist-hip ratio – all boxes ticked. Most breathtaking was her staggering sense of entitlement: there was nothing Courtney did not deserve, could not ask for, was not allowed to say. Fumie and I were in awe of it, never before having met anyone who gave themselves such permissions. Almost as amazing was the fact that Jon found it in any way acceptable; his attitude seemed to be that it came with the territory. It was hard to say which drove us crazier, Courtney's habitual rudeness or Jon's apparent resignation to it.

I could not bring myself to comment on the relationship, the very fact of it being almost too painful to acknowledge. But Fumie badgered Jon relentlessly, as much for his sake as mine, giving voice to all the things I would have liked to have said to him. "She's a cartoon, Jon! Wake up! Stop thinking with your dick for five minutes!" One of Fumie's favourite tactics was to use her phone in restaurants to snap pictures of Jon's face while we all waited for his girlfriend to finish torturing the waiters. "This is you being somebody's bitch," she would say brightly, showing him, and he would flip her off behind his napkin.

Still the Courtney-Jon thing went on. Only once did I ever see him take a stand against her, and it was after a visit where Grace had driven down to meet us for dinner. After her departure Courtney asked, sort of sympathetically, if it wasn't very difficult for me to have a sister as beautiful as Grace. "I mean, I think it would even be hard for *me*," she said, "so I can't imagine what it must be like for *you*."

I looked down at the table. Jon began whispering something to Courtney, who kept saying, "I can't hear you! I can't *hear* you, Jon! Jesus, speak *up*!"

Finally Jon said, full voice, "I was telling you to *think* for once about what you were saying. And if you couldn't accomplish that, to kindly shut the fuck up."

Courtney went into an extended sulk, Jon into an extended silence. Fumie texted him saying *way to grow a pair* and got a black look in return. She took a picture of it.

Later she did her best to comfort me. "Lighten up, Hellie. It's proof the dumb shit isn't completely lost to us. What scares me is that I think that was Courtney's version of empathy."

Oh, but I loved that dumb shit and couldn't give him up. We still got together regularly for one-on-ones where we flogged each other's weak spots to toughen them up. Anatomy for him, biochem for me, genetics for both of us. Courtney didn't like it much, but she didn't care that much, either. She knew that all we were doing was studying, and I didn't count as competition. In her scheme of things I barely counted as female.

Just before finals she mentioned to me that she was leaving for Hawaii immediately afterwards because her cousin was getting married on Maui. Jon would be flying in right after he moved out of his rental, four days later than her but just in time for the wedding. "My whole family's going to be there, so it's the perfect time for him to pop the question," she said. "I'm done with the foot-dragging."

My stomach lurched. I had had no idea that marriage was on the table. Courtney's assuredness meant only that it was something she felt *should* happen, so it was possible that Jon had no idea either. I swallowed hard and asked her why, if she was feeling so impatient, she wouldn't do the asking herself.

No way, she said. She wanted the whole deal: bended knee, open ring box, surprise, tears, onlookers applauding. "I'm handing him the whole setup," she said irritably. "All he has to do is get the ring and *ask*, for God's sake. How hard is that?"

At our next one-on-one I asked Jon if he was looking forward to Hawaii. He stared dully at the table for a while and then said that he was looking forward to it much like you look forward to the speeding train heading straight for you. "So I guess you could say I'm looking *at* Hawaii. Staring it down."

"Then get out of the way," I said. "You've got time."

"Haven't figured out how yet." He grinned weakly. "Bunny in the headlights."

On the afternoon of our last exam I stopped by Jon's house to pick him up. His dad had come down to Guelph to help pack up the contents of the house and take him to the airport, so for once I knocked instead of just walking in. No one answered, so I banged on the door a little harder and waited, cursing Jon in advance for making both of us late.

He'd been walking around looking like he was slated for the gallows, so I guessed that he was going to let the Courtney-train run right on over him. I was furious at him for it and had squandered precious study time frantically trying to think of ways to talk him out of going. I hadn't slept much the night before, hadn't come up with any answers and, stupidly, hadn't given up hope. After a third round of banging and a couple of ill-tempered kicks I lost patience and let myself in.

It's funny how much you can figure out from a very small amount of information. When I walked in the door Jon was standing in the middle of the kitchen saying his own address into his phone in a high, fractured voice. I didn't stop to ask who he was giving the address to in that voice or why, because there could only be one reason. I didn't see Dr. Faulkner in the living room so I went past Jon up the stairs and found his father lying on the floor of the guest room. His suitcase had been tipped off the bed and there were clothes and pill bottles scattered around him. His skin was a dusky grey-blue. I listened to his breathing: long, rattling inhalations, with lengthy gaps in between.

Jon had come up the stairs behind me with 911 on the phone. "Cyanotic," I said, and he nodded and repeated it to the dispatcher. He got down on his father's other side and we began taking turns doing CPR while the dispatcher talked to us. His dad was unresponsive, inert, his colour falling like twilight. Jon's hands were shaking. He kept saying *Dad, come on, Dad, stay with me, stay with me* and I echoed him: *Come on, Dr. Faulkner, stay with us.* I watched his father's eyes turning the grey of a deep, deep bruise but Jon and I kept going, switching back and forth as if we'd been practicing together for months.

When the paramedics came upstairs I told Jon we had to leave him with them, give them room to work. We went downstairs and I helped him find his dad's wallet, coat, shoes. After the paramedics wrangled the gurney down the stairs and into the ambulance they told us they could only take Jon and he wasn't allowed to ride in the back with his dad. Through the front window I watched the ambulance back out of the driveway with Jon sitting in front next to the driver, staring blankly through the windshield.

I watched the ambulance until it rounded the corner and then checked my watch. Thirty minutes to my exam: if I left right then I'd just make it in. Instead I stayed where I was at the window, gazing out over Jon's ratty rented lawn. I'd never seen a person pass away before, but I was fairly sure that Dr. Faulkner was gone. If I went to my exam there wouldn't be anyone here when Jon got back from the hospital. He would come home to the aftermath of what had just happened and be here alone with the fact that his father was dead.

I went up into the spare room and righted the tipped furniture, collected the spilled pills and bottles, picked up the discarded medical supply wrappers that the paramedics had left on the floor. I went back downstairs and put back everything that had been moved aside for the gurney. I cleaned up a plant that had been knocked over and washed the breakfast dishes. Then I sat in the living room and waited.

Jon came home in a cab not quite three hours after he'd left in the ambulance. He'd already called Courtney and told her he wasn't coming. I didn't ask him about his dad because I didn't want to make him say the words. He said them anyway, whispered them because that was slightly less awful than having to say them out loud. I asked him what he needed. Company, he said.

I held his hand while he called his mother and brother and said the awful words out loud for the first time. I held it when we went upstairs to get his and his dad's clothes together. After Jon filled his own bag we packed his dad's suitcase tight and neat. Then Jon put his arms around it and I put my arms around him so that he could cry without having to hold himself up.

We slept in our clothes on the living room floor that night. It was a strange arrangement but he couldn't sleep in his bed. Deep grief and shock take hold of the body like illness in some ways: you can't eat what you normally eat and you can't sleep the same way, either. I held him all night, which was how he wanted it. I'm much smaller than he is but it amazed me how substantial my body felt then, and how he fit inside the circle of my arms. I would not have thought that was possible.

The rest of his family arrived just after dawn, and I thought I should leave so that they wouldn't have to grieve in the presence of a stranger. Jon was in dry shock by then, turning to action to get himself through. He was already on the phone with the funeral home when I left. He caught my hand as I passed him and gave it a hard squeeze. I squeezed back and slipped out the door. He had his family now, and I had to go explain why we'd missed our exam.

I didn't hear from him again until August, when he called my mobile. By then I had a placement at a small clinic in Gananoque. "Where?" Jon laughed.

"You know where," I said. "You drive past it on the way to Ottawa. The casino."

I named the surgeon I was working with and suddenly he knew where I was. He asked me if there were any decent places there for dinner.

We met in Rockport and sat on a patio overlooking the ferry pier, watching tourists feeding French fries to the gulls. Jon was tanned, thinner, remarkably older. He was spending the summer at the cottage outside Ottawa, helping his mom sort things out. Things were all right, he said. Down the road there would be money for him and his brother, and once his loans were paid he might use some of it to start his own practice.

"I'd like to do something commemorative with it," he said. "Something in his honour."

"You will," I said.

He wanted to know what it was like for me there. I understood why he was asking. It was a smaller community without a lot of diversity, and the novelty of Dora might be a bit much.

The first month had been rough, I admitted, but the surgeon I worked with had insisted that everything would be fine. I would reassure clients with my manner and skill, and they would get used to my appearance. She was right on both counts, and by early summer I had already become much more proficient at putting owners at ease. They were always surprised to learn the cause of my injury and often told me that I was very brave to have become a vet.

"Sweet of them," I said to Jon. "But shouldn't I then tell them the truth, that it's got nothing to do with bravery?"

"But you are brave," Jon said. "Until Dad's attack I never thought I'd freeze in an emergency. But if you hadn't been there helping me so calmly I would have been completely paralyzed. Before and after."

"It wasn't my father, Jon. And in the end I couldn't help him."

"Nobody could," he said. "It was too big. But you steadied me. Got me moving."

It was still difficult for him to talk about it. He gripped my hand and we looked out at the water until our food came.

During dinner he told me the thing with Courtney was "very over." She had not thought that his father dying should have prevented him from coming to Hawaii for at least some of their holiday, and he had finally noticed that she was possibly the most selfish person on Earth. He didn't know what he'd do next, but he had to find a placement or risk losing momentum. He wanted to see me, he said, because he needed to see someone from school; that phase of his life had been severed too suddenly. He was glad things with Courtney hadn't gone any further. "Better to find out now," he said, and I had to agree, although it still surprised me that he had lived with it so long.

I wanted there to be more than that, but there wasn't. He was still so sad. We walked after dinner and hugged before getting into our cars. He thanked me again and kissed me on the forehead, a light, dry kiss that no one could possibly misconstrue.

In the car I touched the place and found one of the puncture scars under my fingers. An experiment, to see how it felt to kiss a scar?

Or not. Apparently my hopeful self could misconstrue anything.

⁄ ⁄ ⁄

I startle awake. Jon is kneeling beside the bed, his knapsack on the floor next to him. "Sorry," he says softly. "I was trying not to do that."

He puts his arms around me and I press my face into his neck. Dora, he says into my hair, and I'm struck by the strangeness of the nickname. Does Dora mean me, or my fragmented face? Are we really the same entity to him?

He doesn't want me to walk him out to his car, doesn't want me to get up at all, but I do. In the parking lot he takes my face in his hands.

"Goodbye, Dora," he says very much to her, as if I am not present. His expression brings to mind the faces of owners leaving very sick animals at my clinic. Before they say goodbye they gaze at their pets as if memorizing every mark and twist of fur, and apologize for leaving them to who-knows-what at our hands. That is the look Jon is giving Dora now, as if he is sorry I don't care for her as much as he does.

Finally he lets her go and gives me a fierce, rib-displacing hug. I thank him for coming. He says it's the least he can do.

Just before he pulls out of the parking lot he unrolls his window. "Hellie, you will let me know, right? Whichever way?"

I nod. He is gazing at Dora with that peculiar look on his face again.

"I'll miss her," he says. "I really will."

Shortly after our dinner in Rockport, Jon called to tell me that he'd found a placement in Sudbury, and, incidentally, his first post-Courtney girlfriend. He described Tracey's pros and cons as if she was a car he'd been forced to buy on short notice. I knew it wouldn't last, but it hurt.

After I hung up the phone it kept hurting. Why the meltdown began at that moment, I'll never know; but suddenly that keen, arresting pain became universal acid burning through layer after layer. Everything I'd been holding in check for years was exposed, expanding freely and very much the worse for having been contained under pressure for so long.

Fumie was not home to talk me out of my downward spiral, and once I started circling I descended shockingly fast. By the time I called Grace I was a sad, bleeding, crazy mess, hardly recognizable to either of us. It hurts, I said when she picked up. It hurts.

He could never love me because of how I looked: that was the gist of what I told Grace through wracking sobs. He cared for me, but he would never want me the way I wanted him and it was all Dora's fault. She had not managed to keep me from school or friends or a career, but when it came to attraction the biological imperatives would always win out. No matter how much someone might like me, they would never be able to get past the wrongness of her. The unconscious assumptions I'd held about my future – that someday there would be a long-term partner, someday children – were dissolving in front of me. What there was was what there would be: stares, nervous laughs, whispers of *freak*. Suddenly I could not take another day of it.

"Hellie, come down," Grace said desperately. She couldn't come up because baby Millie had croup. "Come tonight and we'll talk. You're not thinking straight."

The baby's soupy cough in the background made me cry even harder. I couldn't, I said. I had work, I was too upset to drive. For the first time I could not bear the thought of being in Grace's warm little house, spectator to her good marriage and beautiful family.

Grace had always been able to console me before. Now I was truly inconsolable, and it frightened both of us. She did her best over the phone, trotted out all her very best lines about inner beauty and the right person seeing past the exterior and screw 'em anyway, but for the first time they sounded empty. I was heartbroken. Possibly I had been for a long time and was only just then feeling it. I cut her off, saying flatly that nothing short of a new face would help, and then I told her about the list. It touched off the only real argument we had ever had, and it was awful. We became our very worst selves in those few minutes: petty, selfish, accusatory, small.

Grace said that by applying for the list I'd betrayed both of us in the worst way. Oh, she was furious. She said that my reasons for wanting a transplant were shallow, superficial and just plain dumb. I had bought into everything she'd tried to help me fight against and she was sorry she'd wasted her breath. There was nothing wrong with me, and if I didn't trust her on that then why the hell was I phoning her? Jon was a good friend to me, and so *what* if he didn't want anything else. Didn't I know that everyone felt unrequited love? When had I started feeling so damn sorry for myself?

And I sobbed on the other end of the phone and said that she had lied. No matter what I thought of my face or how accustomed to it I became, the world would never get over its strangeness. *She* knew what positive attention was like; *she* knew what it was like to be beautiful. I couldn't even hope for ordinary.

"But you *are* beautiful," Grace said, with such anguish that I knew she meant it.

"You're blind," I said, with a thousand years' bitterness. "You love me and you're blind."

"I'm telling you the truth, Hellie. I'm telling you exactly what I see when I look at you. Is that not good enough?"

No, it was not. Because what good was one person's truth, even if that person was Grace? At that moment I did not have the capacity to believe it was enough.

"What is it that you want so damn much?" Grace said. "What could a different face give you that you don't already have?"

I didn't know. That was part of the anguish: I had been burying and re-burying an enormous sense of loss for years, yet didn't have language for what I might have lost. Of course it wasn't really about my feelings for Jon; those were just the trigger. I had been pushing down an overwhelming sense that there was this enormous other life that would have been, one with so much more possibility. Dora seemed to have limited me in so many ways, and it was only by dint of extraordinary effort that I had anything of my own. What was it like simply to decide on something instead of having to fight for it? Because of Dora, I would never know.

"I didn't choose this," I croaked.

"Listen to me, Helena." Grace's voice was seething with frustration. "*I* didn't get to choose. No one does."

But I was beyond listening. Beyond logic, rebuke, or even kindness.

"*You* have no idea what it's like, *Fortunata*," I said. "You will *never* know."

There was a long silence after that. She was crying and didn't want me to hear her. Finally she surfaced enough to say she had to go but would call me in the morning.

After I hung up then I went and got a bottle from the cupboard. Later on I opened two more. When Grace called at noon the next day I didn't pick up because I was still passed out on the living room floor. She sent me an e-mail instead, and we never spoke about any of those things again.

∅ ∅ ∅

Eight o'clock. Arthur will be calling at ten.

Everything is so hard. For thirty-five minutes I stand in the hotel shower with my forehead against the tile, letting the water pressure do the work of cleansing me. After drying off I try to mobilize the little Fisher-Price coffeemaker but can't remember what order to do things in. I have fresh clothes to put on only because Fumie packed some outfits in an overnight bag for me. My toiletries are here, and she even included my laptop and cell phone charger. Maybe I'll just ask Fumie to pack for me from now on.

As I'm unwinding the laptop's neatly wrapped cord I feel a twinge of longing to see her and Austin. She'll have to get a dog-sitter for him if she comes down for the funeral, whenever that is. Ironically, if I say yes to the transplant Fumie will probably have to go to the service without me.

As I watch the laptop waking up, I recall something I read about face transplant donors: that they aren't left without faces, even if they're being cremated. A silicone facial prosthesis is created from a cast taken before the face is removed, and put in place immediately afterwards. Presumably this lessens the chance of the donor's loved ones being traumatized if the body should be accidentally exposed to them. To us.

I shudder, wishing I hadn't thought of it. In my fantasy transplant scenario there is no body. Grace blesses me from a dream and then I wake up whole, a perfect composite of the two of us. Hellie is finally just Hellie, her new-found symmetry a carefully managed secret. Once the flesh becomes fully innervated there will be no more stares. I'll be so damned normal they'll have to call me Norm.

So call Arthur right now, Hellie. Tell him it's a conditional yes. I dare you.

But there's no part of it that isn't a fantasy. It could be years before I develop good muscle control, and I have a history of grafts not taking well. Despite all the best-case scenario donor conditions being met, I have to assume that something will go wrong. Even if nothing does, I don't know how good a result I can reasonably hope for. A transplant might be my best chance of looking anything like normal, but even Grace's flesh can't give me my might-have-been. Can I live with that? The more I think about it the more paralyzed I feel myself becoming, and ever more resentful of having to make my decision alone.

Jon is afraid that I am waiting to be told what to do. The truth, which is not quite the same, is that I need Grace beside me to steady me and talk me through this. For the last day I have managed to stave off the terrible subject of her absence, but that delay is coming to an end and I am not ready. This can't be all there is. There must be one message more, at least, one last transmission that hasn't reached me yet. My sister would never purposely have left me in this agony of indecision. My sister would never purposely have left me.

Grace sent me a letter the day after we fought about the transplant. It's still here in my email somewhere. At the top she made it clear that she wasn't angry with me, and after I saw that I was so relieved that I scarcely paid attention to the rest.

I pull up my emails from Grace and scroll back, hoping I'll know the subject line when I see it. After hundreds of messages there it is: *Please Forgive Me.*

Dear Hellie,

I sounded so angry with you last night, but I'm not at all. I'm pissed at myself because you are absolutely right – I have no idea what it's like for you. Please, please forgive me for judging you. I had no right to do so.

Did I ever ask her forgiveness for the things I said? I don't remember, but I am ashamed to think that I might not have.

Hellie, here is the truth: I love your face. I love it because it's yours. I look at it and see you, not scars. Everyone who loves you looks at you the same way. But that doesn't automatically mean that you love it too, and you have the right to change it if that's what you want. I will miss the face you have now, but I can learn to love whatever you put in its place.

You're right, looks do matter. They can make things harder or easier in ways that most of us never acknowledge. But I never wanted either of us to put too much stock in our looks because our appearances are far more transitory than we imagine. Neither of us will stay as we are now, and the opinions of strangers won't last either. I don't know what does last, but it isn't anything as frail as a face. That "soul of the body" crap is bullshit, Hellie. A dog tore up your face but your soul's completely intact and it's a good one. No matter what you change, you'll always have that same good soul that I love. So be fearless.

> *Always,*
> *Grace*

At the bottom of the message I notice for the first time that there is an attachment. I click on it and a poem unfurls.

Of course it is Whitman:

Of the terrible doubt of appearances,
Of the uncertainty after all—that we may be deluded,
That may-be reliance and hope are but speculations after all,
That may-be identity beyond the grave is a beautiful fable only,

Grace read *Leaves of Grass* to me over the course of that first summer by Jason's pool, hoping to convey to me what Walt's poems meant to her. This one I heard as I lay with my head on her stomach, feeling the genesis of the breath behind each phrase.

May-be the things I perceive—the animals, plants, men, hills, shining and flowing waters,
The skies of day and night—colors, densities, forms—May-be these are, (as doubtless they are,) only apparitions, and the real something has yet to be known;
(How often they dart out of themselves, as if to confound me and mock me!
How often I think neither I know, nor any man knows, aught of them;)
May-be seeming to me what they are, (as doubtless they indeed but seem,) as from my present point of view—And might prove, (as of course they would,) naught of what they

appear, or naught any how, from entirely changed points of view;

Grace is so close. I can feel her against me, the thrust of her stomach as she laughs.

—To me, these, and the like of these, are curiously answer'd by my lovers, my dear friends;
When he whom I love travels with me, or sits a long while holding me by the hand,
When the subtle air, the impalpable, the sense that words and reason hold not, surround us and pervade us,
Then I am charged with untold and untellable wisdom—I am silent—I require nothing further,

I am terrified of forgetting. Even now I can smell and feel and hear her but I can't bring her face into focus. How did Grace know that it would be the first part of her to fade? Because it is fading, and making her flesh mine won't restore any part of her. Nor will it bring back what I've lost. Have I believed I could shed Dora like an old skin, and all the pain with her? Have I imagined that I could inhabit Grace, and so keep her alive?

The reckoning is upon me. I am waking up to the pain, seeing what a vast and difficult thing mourning my sister will be.

I cannot answer the question of appearances, or that of identity beyond the grave;
But I walk or sit indifferent—I am satisfied,
He ahold of my hand has completely satisfied me.

I understand. What my sister intended, what she hoped I would see. I understand. And only Grace could done this for me; only Grace would have known.

The phone rings, and rings, and rings.

*/ */ */

Most of my free days are spent at what will always be Grace and Jason's house, helping with their daughters. Together with her family I am shifting like a river around the void in our lives, trying to soften its edges. We are surviving, and I know that we will be all right. But grief is such strange, dark territory, and trying to shepherd two young children safely across while navigating it myself sometimes induces in me a depressing sense of helplessness. In my recent dreams Grace is exasperated with our mourning. Stop crying! she keeps saying, but I tell her it's too soon. It's only been six months since we lost you, Gracie. Give us time.

Today the girls and I are up in her study looking at photographs. I lie on the floor with Georgia and Millie draped across my back, turning the album pages for all of us. As we talk they play with my hair, feel the bumps of my old scars, rub their faces against mine. They touch the pictures too, sliding their fingers over each image of Grace as if they might press her back into being.

We study a photo of her smiling from the shallow end of a pool. "She's so pretty," Georgia says with satisfaction, and then puts out her bottom lip when her older sister announces, "*I* look like Mummy. *You* look like Daddy."

"You both look like both," I tell them, and it's true. They change with the angle, like lenticular prints. But Grace-as-child is unmistakably there times two, incarnate for a blink at a time.

There is a snapshot of Grace and me lying together on the lawn in Jason's old backyard. Grace has her nose in *Leaves of*

Grass; it's that summer. I am looking towards the photographer, my face half-hidden behind my hair.

Georgia wants to know what we're doing. "Reading," I tell her. "Your dad must have taken this one."

"Reading a story?"

"Poetry." I point at the Whitman on the shelf. "That one. I read you some of it a few weeks ago, remember? You didn't like it."

"Oh, *that*," Millie sniffs. "It didn't rhyme with anything."

"Poetry doesn't have to rhyme, you know."

"Yes, it does," Millie says with authority, and leans over me to look more closely at the photo. She touches my shadowed expression. "Why weren't you smiling?"

"I couldn't, not properly. And besides, I didn't like having my picture taken."

"Why not?"

"Because I didn't like my face."

"Because the dog bit you?"

"Right. It made me look unusual, and I didn't like that."

She studies my battered Dora-face, weighing this. "Is that why you fixed your smile?"

I do have a fledgling smile now, after years of being unable to lift the left side of my mouth. To replace the atrophied muscle I asked for just one small part of my inheritance from

Grace. It's not a perfectly symmetrical smile yet, but once it's fully innervated it will be close enough. I explained to the girls that it would help make my expressions easier to read, but they couldn't see the point. Why bother with a new smile now, when there were no more reasons to look happy?

I sit up with my back against Grace's desk and gather the girls in. They cling, pressing their cheeks to mine. Together we stare up at the shelves and blue-sky wallpaper and I feel a wave of that same helplessness: where are the words for this *why*? Yes, I wanted to carry something of my sister forward, but the real nature of Grace's gift went far beyond anything physical. How do I convey that we are so much more, and so much more lasting, than our bodies?

I don't know. But we have time. So I will start simply, with what matters most: that I loved their mother's smile, and she left it for me; and now I can smile at them for her.

For nearly six months my contact with Jon has been phone-only because I wanted to surprise him. When we finally connect on Skype and I show him my smile, he is amazed. I'm not sure what he was expecting but he seems hugely relieved.

"Pretty cool, Dora," he says, sounding a little shaky. "Good choice."

For that, after all, was Grace's gift to me: the choice. The chance to understand my first loss so I could find my way through this one.

I ask Jon if he's all right. "Can't explain," he says. "Happy to see you intact."

I look past his shoulder to the room behind him: empty. No ghosts tonight.

"Hey, show me again," he says, and I oblige.

Acknowledgements

Grateful thanks to Quattro Books, particularly to John Calabro, who championed the manuscript and got me around the last bend with wisdom and patience. Maddy Curry's cheerful assistance was also much appreciated.

I am indebted to Meaghan Strimas and my wonderful classmates and instructors in the Creative Writing MFA program at the University of Guelph-Humber. Thanks most of all to Catherine Bush, advisor and story midwife extraordinaire, for her priceless counsel, compassion and faith.

Readers who gave invaluable feedback on early drafts of *Inheritance*: Catherine Bush, Daniel Levinson, Erin Fuller, Mary Running, Laelar Gundlack, Kathy Schildknecht, Christian Gundlack, and Sandra Levinson. Nate Bitton kindly offered helpful insights on childhood injuries, and Jael Richardson provided critical eleventh-hour perspective.

Love and appreciation to my husband Daniel, my mother Mary, and to all those voices of encouragement. You have enabled both the start and the finish.

Other Quattro Fiction